My name is Callum Ormond.
I was undercover on Shadow Island.
My story concludes

ENDGAME

To Dr. David Wood—Inspirationist

First American Edition 2014
Kane Miller, A Division of EDC Publishing

Text copyright © Gabrielle Lord, 2013
Cover design copyright © Scholastic Australia, 2013
Cover design and internal graphics by Nicole Stofberg
Cover logo designed by Natalie Winter

First published by Scholastic Australia Pty Limited in 2013
This edition published under license from Scholastic Australia Pty Limited

Cover photography: Cal's head by Wendell Levi Teodoro (www.zeduce.org) ©
Scholastic Australia 2013; Cal's body and bubbles © istockphoto/Henk Badenhorst;
shark in water with fish, rocks on ocean floor © Peter Hitchins—South West Rocks
Dive Center; boat in water © istockphoto/Dennis Sabo; boat stream © istockphoto/
Bob Thomas; water background © istockphoto/Nastco. Internal photography and
illustration: Hadron Collider on page 060 © istockphoto/glock; Antique key on page
069 © istockphoto/Jimmy Anderson.

For information contact:
Kane Miller, A Division of EDC Publishing
PO Box 470663
Tulsa, OK 74147-0663
www.kanemiller.com
www.edcpub.com
www.usbornebooksandmore.com

Library of Congress Control Number: 2013939416

Printed and bound in the United States of America
1 2 3 4 5 6 7 8 9 10
ISBN: 978-1-61067-172-9

ENDGAME

GABRIELLE LORD

Kane Miller
A DIVISION OF EDC PUBLISHING

PREVIOUSLY...

DAY 30

I escape from Damien's office through a secret hatch and find myself in an underground tunnel system. I find a mysterious laboratory and investigate. There are five rucksacks there containing cryptic information about an upcoming mission for the Zenith team, as well as a box marked *Biosurge*, a pile of modbots and five hologram eyes. I see Damien and Hamish take food for the missing kids who must be being kept somewhere underground.

DAY 31

I rejoin Sophie, Zak and Ariel in their cave. The earthquakes on the island become more frequent and worrying.

DAY 38

To track us down, Damien persuades the resort kids to form search parties to find us. Realizing we need to speed up our plans, we agree that Sophie and Ariel will search the tunnels for the kids that have disappeared while Zak and I head to Delta 11 to see what we can find out about the prisoner there.

DAY 39
Zak and I make it over rough seas to the outcrop. The prisoner's condition is worsening, but I tell him not to lose hope. I manage to report to Paddy at SI-6. Zak and I begin to worry when the girls do not return from their mission.

DAY 40
The girls reappear at our hideout. They think they have made contact with the imprisoned kids underground, but cannot get to them. They've also discovered that the tunnel system reaches all the way to the old cemetery. We now have somewhere else to hide if the search parties find our cave.

DAY 54
In another visit to the underground lab, one of the modbots stings my hand. As I head back to the Katz cave, I'm attacked from behind by somebody. They leave me with a USB containing diagrams of five buildings with skull and crossbones

markings on them. I finally make contact with Boges, who has hacked into Damien's email.

DAY 59

A riddle I received by text message leads me to the old cemetery, where two keys are buried. It seems as though one will unlock the underground prison where the kids are being held—the other one is the key to Delta 11.

DAY 60

Shadow Island is evacuating as the volcano looks set to erupt. The girls go into the tunnels to rescue the kids, but the key breaks in the lock. Zak and I head out to Delta 11 and free the prisoner. Back in the jungle, we come across Georgia Montgomery, one of the elite Zenith team, who is now on the run like us. We head back to the tunnels and break into the underground prison using a mining machine. The volcano threatens to erupt as we wait to be picked up by SI-6, but there's no sign of Ryan. As D'Merrick arrives, she is shot by a sniper. Damien drags Ryan onto the beach and holds us both at gunpoint.

DAY 61

30 days to go . . .

Shadow Island Main Beach

12:01 am

I stood motionless with shock as Ryan twisted and struggled in Damien Thoroughgood's vicious grasp. "Let me go! You can't do this!" Ryan yelled.

I glanced down the beach to our friends—could they help us? But they were too far away in the darkness. I couldn't even see D'Merrick. A shot had rung out and then she had disappeared into the waves. There was no doubting now that Damien would stop at nothing.

Even murder.

I clenched my fists, rage and fear narrowing my field of vision. All I could see was the pistol aimed at my brother's head.

"So, here we are at last," Damien said, pushing Ryan forward with a savage jerk, the eerie light from the volcano revealing the sneer on his face.

I saw with a chill that he had pulled out a

pair of steel handcuffs from his back pocket.

Damien turned his contemptuous gaze on my brother. "You didn't think for a minute that I fell for that fake Gympie Gympie sting routine? I should push you into the nearest Gympie Gympie tree just so you can feel what it's really like." He looked around and my heart froze. Fortunately, it was too dark to see into the dense growth behind the palm trees.

I breathed a sigh of relief as Damien continued to talk to me. "But I was happy to play along. By then I'd checked the security files and seen the two of you together. I knew you wouldn't leave without your brother."

"What do you *want*?" I said carefully.

Thoroughgood paid no attention to my question. "I must say I'm impressed, Cal. The way you lived here undetected, swapping places with your brother so that nobody suspected that there were two of you. But I'm going to need to know everything—who sent you, what you've discovered about Shadow Island and about me. But we can do that at my leisure once I've made your brother comfortable and you've agreed to do what I want."

"Which is what? And what do you mean about Ryan?" I spat out in anger.

We were interrupted by the volcano grumbling to a roar. The explosion of sound was closely followed by a rain of rocks that fell into the sea, hissing. I flinched, my nails digging into my sweaty palms. I felt helpless. I'd failed Ryan and I'd failed SI-6. D'Merrick might be dead. And somehow, I still had to stop Thoroughgood.

I tried to bluff. "Those people getting away on the beach," I said, "they'll get back to the mainland and tell the authorities what's going on here. You'd better let us go and think about saving your own skin!"

Thoroughgood threw back his head, laughing. "Let's get this straight, Cal Ormond. You're the one in trouble here. You *and* your brother. I'll be long gone before anyone gets to Shadow Island. So save your threats—and your strength. You're going to need it to carry out my orders."

"Let go of me, you thug!" yelled Ryan, struggling to escape.

"Shut up! Or I'll give you something to really worry about!" snarled Damien, yanking Ryan hard.

I waited, my guts churning with fear and anxiety. I felt like I was going to be sick. In the orange glow from the volcano, I could see Ryan's eyes were filled with fear. But there was nothing I could do. The deadly muzzle of the pistol was visible just behind my brother's ear.

"One of my Zenith team champions has become, shall we say, *unavailable*, and I need a replacement. That'd be you, Cal. You've proven that you can carry out a complex undercover operation. It shouldn't be too hard for you." He raised his eyebrows and his hard face managed a tight, grim smile. "You will have the honor of carrying out the most dangerous mission of all."

"No way!" The words were out before I could bite them back.

"Oh, yes. You're the perfect solution. You will take his place at the seventh experiment. And if you don't—" A cruel jab of the pistol into Ryan's neck made my brother flinch. I stifled a yell. I had to stay calm for Ryan's sake.

I played for time while my brain went into overdrive trying to think of a way to save us both. "OK! OK. I'll do what you want. But what's the seventh experiment?"

Damien smiled. "That's the big one, Cal. Shut down by shortsighted idiots because it was ahead of its time. It needs someone with vision and a real intellect. And I'll be waiting to hear all about it at land sighting where no one can possibly find . . ." He stopped, suddenly aware of saying too much.

I was astounded at his contempt for other people and his massive ego. I focused on keeping him talking, hoping some idea would occur to me. "What do you mean? If no one can find you, how can I find out what my mission is? Once I get to the mainland, you'll tell me then?"

"You'll know everything in good time. But for now you can run along. Join your friends on the beach."

"But I don't know what to do! How can I carry out this—this—operation if I don't know what you're talking about?"

"A rucksack will be sent to you—it will have instructions. And now, I'm taking your brother with me. He's my guarantee that you will do exactly as I say. And of course you won't do anything silly like informing the authorities, will you? *Because I will know.* And your brother will pay."

"You can't keep Ryan here!" I said, as a huge explosion blew from the top of the mountain and red-hot lava started sliding down the slopes. The smell of burning wood and the heat from the volcano filled the air. Choking fumes were starting to settle around us.

"*I* give the orders," Damien snapped, keeping his eyes on us as he reached behind him, tucking the pistol into the back of his belt and then clapping one half of the handcuffs around Ryan's left wrist. This scared me more than I could say. It must have scared Ryan too because instinctively he struggled, twisting away. Although he was no match for Damien, he cracked open a moment of opportunity which I'd hoped for.

With all the force in my body, I hurled myself at Damien as he reached over to seize Ryan's flailing right arm. Damien, taken completely by surprise, stumbled. Before he could regain his balance, I grabbed Ryan's arm, and yanked him away from Damien's grip, the handcuffs swinging wildly.

We bolted—we were free! Behind us, I heard Damien take off after us. Then I heard him stumble again. Without losing my stride, I glanced back. Damien had tripped on a tree root and was scrambling to get up.

This gave us even more precious time. I didn't have to urge my brother to run faster. Within seconds, he'd overtaken me!

I broke every personal record for speed as we hurtled down the beach. The volcano was spewing fumes and sulfurous smoke, making breathing difficult. The fumes burned in my nose and at the back of my throat. I could feel hot ash falling onto my head. The air was heating up, even down here on the beach. All the while, I expected to hear bullets whizzing past our heads.

Risking another backward glance, I turned around, but Damien was nowhere to be seen. He hadn't followed us down the beach to the others. *Coward.*

In the distance I could make out the others at the end of the long beach, huddled away from the blazing spotlight. What was going on? *Are they gathered around the lifeless body of D'Merrick?* Then came another thought, almost as terrifying. *How had Thoroughgood known that D'Merrick was coming?* The only people who knew about it were on our team . . .

I ran harder, shouting to them now. They were crowding around an inflatable near the shore-line. I thought I caught a glimpse of D'Merrick's gleaming hair. But she'd been shot, *hadn't she?*

I gasped as the brilliant spotlight swung across the sand and caught my friends in its searching beam, lighting them up like ornaments on a Christmas tree.

"Oh no!" Ryan shouted. "They're sitting ducks!"

Shots rang out and my worst fears were confirmed. Damien had ordered the sniper in the tower to fire at my friends!

12:04 am

But as the last echoes of the shots faded, the brilliant light suddenly vanished and the beach was plunged into darkness. Maybe the volcanic eruptions had interfered with the power. At least we'd have the cover of darkness while we made our escape.

As we reached the others, I was shocked but utterly relieved to see no one else had been hurt, and that D'Merrick was very much alive and hastily overseeing the loading of the two inflatables, a pistol clenched in one hand. "I thought you were dead!" I said. "You were shot. I saw it!"

"I'm pretty hard to kill, Cal. It's a flesh wound; I'll be all right," D'Merrick said, brushing my concern aside.

"That looks painful," I said, looking at the seeping bandage on her arm.

"I fell out of the inflatable and hoped that the shooter would think I was a goner," she replied.

"And then Ariel took out that searchlight," Zak added.

Ariel shrugged as if to say it was no big deal.

"Somebody tipped Damien off," I said. "Somehow he knew exactly when you were going to arrive here. How could that happen?"

D'Merrick shook her head. "Not now, we're exposed here, it's time to get off this island. Let's go."

Dr. Freeman, Sabina, Quan and Artemiz got into the first inflatable, Sophie climbing in after them. Dr. Freeman hunched up at the back while Sophie took the tiller and the outboard engine roared into life. D'Merrick gestured for me and

Ryan to get into the second inflatable, along with her, Georgia, Zak and Ariel. That's when we realized there was only room for one more. Either me or Ryan—but not both.

"Get in, Ryan," I said.

"No, *you* get in," he said.

"Come on, Ryan. Stop wasting time," I insisted.

"No way am I going without you. Deal with it. OK?" Ryan's face was set.

Zak and Ariel both stood up and the inflatable rocked dangerously. "We'll get out. We've survived on this island for months. We can be picked up later," Ariel said.

The volcano interrupted our argument as geysers of fire exploded skyward and piles of thick ash cloud climbed above it into the night sky. The molten lava sliding down the mountain would soon make its way through the gullies in the rainforest.

"Zak and Ariel, sit down. Ryan and Cal, stop arguing," ordered D'Merrick. "You'll both fit in fine. Come on, try."

But when we did, the inflatable sagged into the water with barely an inch above the waterline. I'd spent a lot of time around boats and I knew that even a moderate wave would swamp the inflatable. It was too dangerous. "It's overloaded, D'Merrick, you know it."

The first boat was already pulling away, its outboard churning up the sea. D'Merrick stood up, rocking the second inflatable. "Look," she said. "*I'll* stay. You guys must get away safely. I'll call BB and he'll be able to guide you to the pickup point."

As she spoke, the beach shuddered and a small wave rippled on the sea.

"No," I said. "What if BB doesn't get the message? We'll take Damien's submersible. I know where it is."

I felt Zak staring at me and I knew he was going to mention the electronic padlock. I gave him a warning look and there was enough light from the volcano for him to see it.

D'Merrick looked hesitantly at the other departing inflatable. "OK, I'll have to go," she said, with reluctance. "The others don't know how to calibrate the coordinates. I need to be with them."

"*Go!* It's OK," I reassured her. "Remember how I passed all your tests? We'll be fine, won't we, Ryan?"

"Yes," said my brother defiantly.

"OK, then. Good luck," said D'Merrick, starting the outboard.

I watched for a few moments as they pulled away from the beach. I wasn't as sure as I'd sounded. We had to get to the mooring cave and start the submersible before Shadow Island became a volcanic tomb, just like a modern-day Pompeii.

For a moment I stood, undecided. There was the motorboat, but we didn't have the key. And Damien would surely have taken it. Maybe it would be better to grab the raft and get away on that. But where would we go? Rowing into the darkness, not knowing where we were, without water and food, could be the end of us. We would have to try the submersible—there was no other way.

Ryan and I ran down the beach, heading for the south end and the rocks that surrounded the mooring cavern. If I'd been scared before, I was really scared now.

Every few moments there was another earthquake and another terrifying growl from the volcano. Even out in the open air of the beach, we were coughing and spluttering and had pulled our T-shirts up around our mouths hoping to filter out the worst of the fumes.

We made it to the rocks that stood like sharks' teeth in the boiling surf. I wasn't looking forward to navigating my way around those. What if we couldn't get into the submersible at all . . .

I looked back at the volcano. As I watched it, another huge wave of hot smoke and ash billowed up and out and started rolling down the gullies.

"Ryan! Quick! We've gotta get into the cave before that hot smoke reaches down here or we'll be cooked!" I yelled, as we started to navigate the crashing surf and sharp volcanic rock towards the mooring cavern. I feared every wave would deliver the fatal sting of an Irukandji jellyfish carried in its surge. Shadow Island was now violently hostile—poisoning the air, pushing us towards the jagged rocks and threatening us with the deadly and invisible strands of the fatal jellyfish.

Finally, we made it past the last of the drenching waves and dangerous rocks and came to the overhanging cavern entrance. *With not a minute to spare*, I thought, as we hurled ourselves through the opening and into the relative shelter of the huge cave.

Mooring Cavern

12:28 am

We made it just in time. Outside, the world became darker as volcanic ash and debris surged down the mountainside and into the sea, hissing and spitting. Steam drifted into the cave where we huddled.

We stumbled through the darkness to where the submersible, barely visible apart from tiny highlights on the polished fittings, rocked at its mooring. Did the fact that it was still here mean that Damien might still be on the island? He could be making his way through the tunnels right now! But I could not see the other boat. Maybe he had already made his escape. I pushed those thoughts aside as we ran to the bobbing submersible. It lay like a sleek javelin, all glass and polished chrome. I pulled out my phone and shone a sharp light onto the door of the cabin. My heart sank as I saw that above the gleaming handle the electronic lock was still there.

I looked closer, puzzled. The keypad was made up of letters, not numbers. I'd never seen a lock like this—Damien must have designed it himself.

I groaned.

"That's going to be tough to crack!" said Ryan.

"Thanks a lot. I wouldn't have figured that out myself," I snapped.

Small stones started falling down from the roof of the cave. "The roof is starting to collapse!" Ryan yelled, ducking away as an airborne stone grazed the side of his face.

I shone the beam from my flashlight app up to the roof of the cavern. A jagged crack had appeared in the rocky ceiling. The earthquakes caused by the volcanic activity were affecting the hollowed-out underworld of Shadow Island. As I watched, the crack grew wider.

Any moment now, the whole cave could collapse in on itself, burying us and the submersible deep underground. I shivered at the thought. But we couldn't get out of there until we'd figured out the keypad code.

"I've never seen one like this," said Ryan, peering at the letters.

On an impulse, I pushed the three R buttons in succession. Nothing.

"It wouldn't be that simple," said Ryan.

"I don't know," I said. "So many people have a password like 1, 2, 3, 4. Or A, B, C, D. Or those sequences backward."

"How about the first four, then?" said Ryan, pushing U R H D. Nothing happened. He pushed them again in the reverse order. Still nothing.

There was another rumble and another shower of grit and rocks hit the water, bouncing off the boat. Ryan jumped back from the keypad lock. "Cal! We've gotta get out of here! Do we have a Plan B?"

I didn't answer him, too intent on trying out different combinations.

"What about bashing in the windshield?" Ryan suggested, looking around for something heavy.

"It's a watertight cabin," I said. "It rides quite low in the water. Breaking the windshield could make it sink once we get out into the open sea."

A huge rock fell from the center of the cave, creating a massive splash that rocked the submersible and completely soaked us. This cave could turn into a deathtrap at any moment, I realized. But outside, the air was filling with poisonous fumes and deadly lava slides. I felt panic starting to clutch at my guts. We had to find a way into this boat!

I tried to concentrate, focusing on the letters themselves, trying to make words out of them. Maybe that was the key. I blinked, as suddenly something registered.

"Hey, Ryan . . . I've just noticed something! These letters!" I yelled with excitement. "They make a word. Look, you can type the word MORDRED!"

"Quick! Try that! That's *got* to be it."

It wasn't.

A terrifying crack of thunder turned out to be a whole section of the cavern roof breaking away and crashing into the sea near the entrance to the cave. The boat rocked violently and we were soaked once more. I could feel the fear and panic increasing—my breath came in short sharp gasps; my heart was racing. *Stay calm,* I told myself. *Stay calm and do the next sensible thing.* OK. So it wasn't the word Mordred. But odds were it was a word—a word connected to Damien. So what could it be? My brain raced. I quickly scanned the letters. What other words could I make with the letters?

Of course! "I've got it!" I said, punching in the six letters.

With a click, the lock turned.

"*Yes!*" Ryan yelled as we tumbled inside. "What was the password?"

"Arthur," I said, still baffled by Damien's obsession with the legend of King Arthur and Mordred. Maybe one day it would all make sense. *Did he think he was some kind of king?*

12:35 am

We scrambled into the cabin. I strapped myself into the pilot's seat and switched on the ignition.

Beside me, Ryan buckled up in the first officer's seat. The engine roared into life and the whole boat trembled at the power surge.

Powerful headlights lit up, revealing more cracks in the roof of the cave. I winced as heavy rocks fell on top of the cabin. The noise was deafening and I feared that a big rock would break through the transparent roof of the craft and damage it—and us. I didn't have time to figure out anything except how to start and steer this amazing boat. I activated the GPS function and chose the last selected coordinates, praying that Damien's most recent trip in it had been to the mainland. Within seconds, the computer had set our course.

Leaving a rush of white water behind us, the boat edged its way to the cavern opening, gathering speed. As we surged through the natural archway that formed the entrance to the open sea, the submersible was jolted as a huge rock hit the top of the cabin, knocking the sleek craft sideways. It righted itself quickly, then over-corrected. I gripped the wheel, trying to stop the bucking vehicle from crashing into the edge of the archway. Finally, I managed to bring it under control and steer it through safely.

"I just hope that rock hasn't damaged the boat," I said. "Check the canopy, will you? I have to concentrate on navigating around these rocks."

Ryan undid his seatbelt and twisted around, his hands moving over the low canopy of the submersible's cockpit. "It's OK, I think," he said. "There's no damage. It all seems fine to me."

Once outside the cave, the submersible picked up speed, pushing through the waves. I was going to need all my boat skills and a bit of luck to avoid the dangerous needles of rock. The sea around us reflected the garish red light coming from the volcano. It looked as if we were riding through a surging sea of black and crimson.

We were heading straight for a vicious-looking upthrust of black rock, with angry surf foaming around it. Frantically, I tried to steer away from it, but the steering was locked. We were going to crash straight into it!

Ryan gasped in fear. I braced myself for the crash. But something amazing happened! The submersible veered away at the last moment, speeding safely past. Then I saw the steering wheel move by itself and realized that the boat had radar and autopilot. It had detected the steeple-shaped rock!

As the submersible weaved its way past more menacing rocks, I felt myself relaxing for the first time in hours. The incredible boat was doing all the work. We'd gotten away from Shadow Island before it blew up. We were free!

As we sped past the coastline, heading for home, Ryan and I stared through the window at the island. Rivulets of fire were streaming down the mountainside and falling into the sea, creating huge clouds of steam and boiling water around them. It was unbelievable, but we'd escaped.

"We did it!" Ryan shouted in excitement, giving voice to my thoughts. "We got away and we got everybody out. Whatever Damien's plan is, we've spoiled it now."

I wasn't so sure, but I didn't want to rain on my brother's parade.

"What about Damien and Hamish?" Ryan suddenly asked. "We've got the submersible. I wonder if they'll be able to escape?"

I shrugged. "They might have taken the motorboat. I'm sure they know how to take care of themselves," I said, "and right now, after Damien threatening you like that, worrying about his welfare is pretty low down on my list of priorities."

Shadow Island Coastline

12:41 am

Out on the open sea, the boat looped through the

waves with an exciting lift and thud, just like the dolphins it had been modeled on. Behind us, the outline of Shadow Island was fading into a dim blur against the horizon, with its volcanic furnace glowing red in the distance.

Confident now that the boat was piloting us safely home, I turned to my brother. His grin was as wide as mine. The excitement of speed, the beauty of the night sky above us and, best of all, the fact that we were free at last, was exhilarating!

I turned my attention to a switch on the dash-board which was labeled: *Activate Dive Function*. I slid my phone into the watertight compartment in front of me, just in case. "Let's go diving," I said, flicking the switch.

As I did so, the submersible sank gently beneath the waves and a searchlight at the front shone a cone of white light into the black water ahead of us. We were only a few feet down, but already I could feel the pressure against my ears. The dive function leveled us out and we were now speeding along under the waves, away from the turbulence of the surface.

As we speared through the water, it seemed as if the sea was parting before us. We were surrounded by curtains of dark water. In the brilliance of the searchlight, schools of fish sped past us and disappeared in a silvery flash down into the depths. A huge blue groper blinked up at us from below as we passed him by. Shrimp-like creatures glowed with rainbow colors as the light hit them, before disappearing in a blur of iridescence. It was a magical underwater journey.

I noticed on the speedometer that the under-water function slowed our progress, so after we'd enjoyed swimming with the fish for a couple of minutes, I deactivated the dive function and the submersible started to gently rise towards the surface once more. I looked downward, sorry to be leaving.

A huge, dark shadow loomed up out of the depths, the gray-and-white markings and the torpedo shape unmistakable. A shudder went through me as I reminded myself that we were safe in the cabin of the submersible. Higher and higher the shark swam towards us—a gigantic great white—the top predator in the ocean.

Crack!

"What the—!" The rest of my words were washed out of me as a massive dump of water crashed over my head. I looked up in horror! The roof of the canopy gaped wide and the ocean was pouring in. Whatever had crashed on top of the cabin as we left the mooring cave must have left an invisible crack which had burst open from the underwater pressure. I had to bring the submersible up to the surface as quickly as possible or we'd both drown! I turned to my brother, but Ryan had disappeared! Without his seatbelt on, the rush of water must have carried him out into the ocean through the gaping hole. The water was threatening to cover the controls on the dashboard and the weight of it was pushing down the nose of the submersible.

I gasped in terror when the glaring searchlight illuminated the massive shark almost on top of us! *Where was Ryan?* I had to get him out of the water!

I lifted the nose of the boat up and up until it broke the surface of the ocean. As the water started to drain out, I battled to lock the steering wheel to force the boat into a tight circle. When the submersible started turning, its brilliant light picked up the small figure of my brother, desperately swimming towards the circling craft.

Without thinking, I jumped into the water to meet him, grabbing a boat hook I'd seen secured in the bottom of the boat. I wasn't sure if he'd spotted the shark, but when the light from the submersible flashed over him, the expression on his face told me that he had!

"Ryan! Ryan! Hurry!" I shrieked, seeing a huge dorsal fin break the surface behind him. As Ryan swam desperately towards the boat, I lashed out with the hook, splashing the water near the shark, hoping to scare it off. "Get into the boat!" I screamed at my brother.

The light made another eerie circle around us as I treaded water, the metal hook raised and ready. Ryan grabbed onto the side of the submersible and hauled himself halfway out of the water as he tried to scramble back into the moving cabin. Behind him, the huge shark rose in the water and I saw that it was almost as big as the twenty-foot boat! It sank beneath the waves, but the dorsal fin, still visible, sped up. The shark was heading straight for my brother's legs!

"Get in, Ryan! *Get in!*" I screamed over the noise of the motor while striking out towards the circling boat. But Ryan was in trouble, unable to haul himself completely inside, and now the shark rose towards the surface, only a few feet ahead of me and close behind my brother. With all my strength I lunged as far as I could and smashed the boat hook across the top of the shark's back. It rolled, its fins thrashing the water, and then disappeared.

It was worse *not* knowing where it was. I saw with relief that Ryan was finally fully inside the broken cabin. He grabbed the steering wheel and aimed the submersible straight at me. But it was too late—I sensed the shark coming up behind me and flung myself across the last arm's length of water to the boat, but as Ryan reached out to me I felt a tug on my leg, and then suddenly I was pulled under the waves—the shark had me!

I thrashed wildly as the beast dragged me down, its teeth beginning to sink into my right leg. The pain made me scream and I lost my last breaths of air. Panic overwhelmed me—how could I escape those jaws?

The boat hook!

With my last strength I wrenched the hook across my body and slammed it into the shark's flank. It yanked out of my grasp as it stuck in the rough flesh. I felt the shark's jaws open for a split second, but it was all I needed.

Lungs bursting, I pushed up to the surface. I exploded out of the water, and like some kind of miracle, Ryan's hand came out of nowhere and grabbed my arm, dragging me painfully inside. Blood poured from my leg into the waterlogged cabin as I gasped and spat out salty water.

"He's not gone yet!" Ryan yelled, turning to the controls. The submersible was savagely rammed by the shark, almost pushing it over onto its side.

"Step on it!" I screamed. Immediately, we shot forward so fast that I banged my head on the dashboard. We sped through the black water in grim silence, the only sounds our heaving breaths.

It wasn't until we'd put a good distance between us and the great white that we even spoke.

"I've never swum so fast in my life," said Ryan. "I thought I was a goner. And then you disappeared . . ." he trailed off.

"I know . . ." I sighed. "That was pretty intense." I leaned over and pulled up my pant leg to view the damage. We both winced to see the bite wounds.

"Nice scars you're going to have to add to your collection," Ryan said.

"Thanks to you, I'm here to tell the tale," I said quietly. I gave him a fierce hug. "I won't forget it."

"Right back at you, bro," Ryan smiled.

12:55 am

A few minutes later, we had a new worry. A lot of water was leaking into the cabin and we didn't have anything to bail it out. We'd escaped from an erupting volcano, gotten away from the ruthless Damien Thoroughgood *and* a hungry shark, but now we seemed to be in danger of sinking. It was time to call in the cavalry. Silently congratulating myself for keeping my phone safe, I called SI-6.

"Cal! Where are you? D'Merrick just called. We've been waiting to hear from you. Are you all right?" BB said.

It was hard to hear him because of the wind rushing through the broken canopy of the submersible and I was still too shaken to talk about the shark—there'd be time for that later. My leg throbbed and my side was starting to hurt where Ryan had dragged me into the boat.

Instead I only said, "Great to talk to you!" giving Ryan the thumbs up. "We're in a submersible, but it's taking in water. It's a slow leak, but I'm not sure we'll make it to the mainland."

"Give me your speed and your GPS coordinates," BB said.

I did so while Ryan looked at me expectantly. "What's he saying?" he hissed at me.

I nodded, listening to BB. "See you soon," I said, hanging up.

"Well?" Ryan said.

"BB's sending an Otter," I said, trying not to laugh at the confused expression on Ryan's face. "He's sending a sea plane—it's a single-engine plane called an Otter. They'll rendezvous with us within the hour."

"Let's hope we can stay afloat till then," said Ryan.

1:48 am

Sure enough, less than an hour later, we saw the bright lights of the plane. Ryan stuck one of the flares we'd found in the submersible's water-tight compartment into the air and yanked on the wire ignition pull. Almost immediately, the surrounding sea was lit up with a bright red light. Now we could plainly see the de Havilland Otter coming in low over the water, the pilot putting it down neatly on the choppy surface and altering its course a little, guided by the red flare.

I steered the submersible as close as I could without banging into the Otter's floats. The flare died down as the cockpit door opened.

Axel's face appeared. "Hey, guys!" he grinned. "Come on board! Great to see you both safe at last."

Another face appeared behind Axel's. I couldn't believe my eyes. My best friend had come along for the ride. "Hey, dude! Hey, Ryan!" Boges called out. "Had enough fun on the island, then? Whoa! what happened to your leg, Cal?"

We climbed into the plane, helped by Axel and Boges, and crammed ourselves into the seats at the back. Once my leg had been bandaged, Axel gunned the engine for takeoff and Boges turned around to say, "Now that you're both stowed on board—tell me everything!"

So we did just that.

After taking it all in, Boges finally said, "You going to call Winter? She'll want to know you're OK."

"Yeah," I said, "a bit later."

"We've both learned from experience that she doesn't appreciate early-morning interruptions to her beauty sleep, eh, dude?" Boges laughed. Then he frowned.

"Why do you have a handcuff bracelet, Ryan?" Boges asked.

"That's how everyone's wearing them this season," Ryan joked.

Dolphin Point Marina

2:40 am

Axel put the sea plane down smoothly and Paddy was waiting for us with a small speedboat.

I looked at Axel and then Paddy. "Don't you guys ever sleep?"

"Sleep's for babies," grinned Axel. "Instructions are to take you both back with us to HQ where you can clean up a bit. You can't go home looking like that."

I looked at Ryan, then at myself. I realized we looked as if we'd been living outside for months, been chased through a jungle, covered in dirt and then drowned at sea. *Which is kinda what happened.*

"I take your point," I said, laughing.

"You look like a pair of zombies—and as for the *smell* . . ." Boges added, earning himself a punch in the arm.

At the jetty, we all transferred into a car driven by Paddy, who drove Boges home.

SI-6 Headquarters
Clayton Morris Industrial Estate

3:29 am

As we arrived at SI-6, BB rushed outside to greet us and shook our hands warmly. But when I told him about our dangerous escape from Shadow Island and the great white shark, he visibly paled.

"Thank goodness," he said finally, "that you made it home safely. Axel will show you where you can get showered and changed. You'll find some new clothes waiting for you. I think it's about time your families saw you, but at least you can rest here and get some sleep until a more reasonable hour. But then we'd like you to come back tomorrow for a debriefing session. OK?"

I nodded. "Of course, I understand," I said.

"First though, I just want to thank you for bringing Sophie safely home. And you too, Ryan," he continued, turning to him. "You both risked your lives for my daughter and I will never forget that."

I hadn't really seen it like that before. The way I looked at it, I'd set off to find Ryan and without really meaning to, had discovered a whole new world of danger.

Home
Flood Street, Richmond

10:52 am

I had to admit it was great to be home. What a reunion! Mum was thrilled to have me back again and when Ryan walked in behind me, she wrapped her arms around him as well. Gabbi came hurtling down the stairs and threw herself into the group hug, almost knocking us over.

I explained to Mum how after finishing my elite flight school apprenticeship I'd gone on to Shadow Island to meet up with Ryan.

"That's right, Mrs. O," Ryan chimed in. "And then we decided to come home together."

I told her quite a bit about Shadow Island, but naturally I left out the bits I knew would turn her hair white—the volcano, the imprisoned kids, Damien's evil plans, as well as the twenty-foot great white. As far as Mum was concerned, Ryan had been enjoying himself at a resort and I'd met up with him there. She scolded Ryan a little for leaving so abruptly, but she was so happy to have him back safely she couldn't stay mad for long. "You must let your other mum know right away," Mum said.

"I've spoken to her already, Mrs. O. I called her earlier," said Ryan. "She's at work at the moment."

We were interrupted by the arrival of Winter who'd mustered herself very quickly after my call. She raced into the kitchen, halted, and put her hands on her hips, raising an eyebrow.

"Nice threads," she said, admiring my new T-shirt. "And look at Ryan. Don't you two look awesome?"

I grinned and asked, "Is that all I get?"

"How about this?" she asked, kissing me as I threw my arms around her and lifted her up in a tight embrace.

She stepped back, looking into my eyes. "Welcome home! How was super-cool flight school and the tropical island?"

"We learned a lot, didn't we, Ryan?" I said, my grin getting wider.

"Heaps," said Ryan. "Ocean swimming is my new specialty!"

Our eyes met and for a moment the jokey atmosphere changed.

"How about some food? I'm starving!" I said to

cover up the awkwardness.

Then we all got in the way while Mum cooked up a huge late breakfast of sausages, grilled tomatoes, toast and eggs.

When there was a break in the heavily censored conversation about Shadow Island, Gabbi looked at both of us suspiciously. "Why do I have the feeling that there's something going on that we don't know about?" she asked.

I grabbed her and tickled her until she squealed. She tried to tickle me back, but I held her off. Winter sprang to her aid and fortunately Gabbi's question was forgotten in the general craziness. My little sister is too smart sometimes.

Winter's House
Mansfield Way, Dolphin Point

9:04 pm

After spending the day with our families, we found ourselves back at Winter's place later that night. Stretched out on the couch, with the others opposite me in the spacious living room, Ryan and I told Winter and Boges about the events leading up to our escape from Shadow Island. Ryan reveled in all the terrifying details of our encounter with the shark. Boges and Winter listened in shocked silence.

"It almost got him," I said. "And then the next thing I knew, it was dragging me under."

"Oh my goodness!" Winter cried, after I'd told them the whole story. "It could have killed you. Even for *you* that's a narrow escape," she added quietly.

No one said anything for a while.

"Well, now SI-6 can chase Damien and you guys can get some rest," said Boges, a thoughtful look on his face. "Did I tell you SI-6 have asked if I'd like to keep working for them?" he said. "On the Mordred key?"

Winter laughed, digging him in the ribs. "I know why you said yes."

"Because I can do it, Winter. And they recognize my brilliance," he said.

"It's your modesty, Boges," she teased, "that's what they're attracted to. And I think *your* attraction might be more to do with a certain Miss Maxine Flint . . . look, you're blushing!"

It was true. Boges's round face was flushed.

"I don't blush!" he said, his face crimson.

"Who's Maxine Flint?" I asked.

"The head of the section where Boges is working," said Winter. "She's a bit of a fox, eh, Boges?"

"Whoo-hoo!" I said. "Tell us more, Boges!"

"She's really smart, thank you very much," he said, with a frown.

"She's really *hot*," said Winter, nudging him and me.

"Ouch!" I said, as she did so.

"What is it?" she asked.

"More narrow-escape injuries," I said, pulling up my T-shirt. Even I was impressed. A huge, purple-red bruise covered my entire right side, punctuated with patches of blackish-red where my skin had been grazed on the sharp edges of the splintered canopy as Ryan had pulled me back into the boat.

"Ouch is right!" Boges said.

I pulled the T-shirt down again. I'd almost forgotten something. I'd brought along the blister pack of Biosurge that I'd taken from the underground laboratory back on Shadow Island.

"You said you had a mate in the university chemistry department, Boges. Can you give him this, please?"

"Is this the Biosurge stuff you mentioned?" said Boges, taking it from me.

"We're pretty sure it contains some kind of performance-enhancing drug. It was given to the Zenith team, Damien's elite 'athletes' once they got to the very top level. Then they got the 'Z' tattoo and the implant."

"I'll talk to my friend, Alistair," said Boges. "He won't mind running some tests on it."

After Boges and Ryan had left, Winter and I chatted a bit longer, but I could feel my eyelids getting heavy.

"I've got a meeting with BB tomorrow morning," I said. "He wants me to give him a full briefing on everything I discovered on Shadow Island."

"What is it, Cal? I can tell there's something worrying you," Winter said, almost reading my thoughts.

I shook my head. "It's probably nothing. But I can't help feeling I haven't heard the last of Damien Thoroughgood."

Next thing I knew, Winter was gently shaking me awake. "Cal, Cal . . . time for bed."

"Huh?" I pulled myself upright on the couch.

"Don't get up, I texted your mum and told her you were crashing on the couch here," she whispered. "Get a good night's sleep," she said after a pause, kissing me good night.

I didn't have the energy to argue with her. As I sank back into the soft cushions my whole body ached from all it had been through on Shadow Island—sleeping outside, scraping together enough food each day, being constantly on alert and in fear. The weeks of hardship seeped through my bones as I slipped into a dreamless sleep.

DAY 62

29 days to go . . .

SI-6 Headquarters
Clayton Morris Industrial Estate

9:22 am

The next morning, I was picked up in an unmarked car driven by Paddy. I barely recognized him dressed in a dark suit and tie.

As he drove, Paddy asked me a lot of questions. I tried to answer him without giving too much away because until I'd spoken to BB, I didn't know how much I should say about anything.

We pulled up outside SI-6's headquarters in the industrial estate and I headed straight through the glass doors. Paddy pointed to a door. "You'll find them in the conference room down there."

Before I reached it, the door opened and I saw BB beckoning me. As I walked inside, I saw D'Merrick with her arm in a sling and Axel with his cheeky grin and cropped hair, both sitting at a long table.

Axel pulled out a chair for me. "Take a seat, Cal," he said, as BB sat down opposite. I did so and looked expectantly at the others.

"How's the flesh wound?" I asked D'Merrick.

"Sore. But I'm a big girl," she grinned.

BB leaned over to switch on a computer recording program. "So we don't have to take notes and you don't have to repeat yourself later," he smiled. Then he folded his hands on the table. "Right, Cal. As you can imagine, we're eager to hear about your time on Shadow Island. Please start at the very beginning when you landed and leave nothing out. Even something that seems like an insignificant detail could turn out to be useful."

It took quite a while to tell them everything that had happened, including how I'd eventually freed Sophie and my concern about whatever it was that Damien was plotting.

"We examined the diagrams of those unknown buildings that you sent through to us," said BB, "and one of our analysts recognized the layout of the one in Hong Kong. He's worked in security there and identified the diagram as the service office for the electrical grid for the whole of Hong Kong."

I frowned. "Why would Damien be interested in that building?"

BB explained. "An attack on the computers that service the electrical flow in a big city would be absolutely disastrous. We're desperately trying to find what the other four targets might be. But let's hope that's not going to happen." He sighed and I thought how heavily burdened BB must be.

"Damien is very dangerous—more dangerous than we had ever suspected." He paused again. "When did you last see him?"

"On the beach after he'd tried to kidnap Ryan—we took off and he seemed to just disappear. I don't know what happened to him," I added. "I can't even be sure he got off the island. Or what happened to his second-in-command, Hamish."

BB looked at the others before answering. "We know that Thoroughgood *did* get away. He must have taken the motorboat you mentioned or possibly a helicopter hidden somewhere on the island. We know he got back to the mainland because he accessed his bank accounts."

"Why don't you just arrest him when you find him?" I asked, puzzled.

BB leaned forward across the table. "We believe that Thoroughgood is planning a massive crime—a crime of international dimensions—but if we arrest him now, we might not be able to stop what he has planned being carried out. But if we can find him, we can watch him first and see what he does."

"Maybe I could help," I said, almost thinking aloud. "Damien wanted me to work for him. I could offer to do that and discover what he's up to and get information back to you."

BB frowned and shook his head. "Being a double agent is terribly dangerous, Cal," he said. "I'd even think twice about using one of our very experienced agents for that sort of work. You're home now, so let's keep you safe. So was there anything else?"

"I think that's it," I said. I shrugged. "How is everyone, by the way?"

"Thanks to you, some very anxious parents have been reunited with their children. We're having a meeting with them and the minister for defense. The parents and the kids all understand the need for complete secrecy about the investigation we're undertaking into Damien Thoroughgood."

"And how about Georgia?" I asked.

"She was with us when we got to the mainland," answered D'Merrick, swinging her thick braid back behind her shoulder. "But she split sometime after that."

"There were a lot of people milling around," Axel said.

D'Merrick nodded. "I feel bad that she disappeared on my watch."

"Don't feel bad," I said. "Her nickname was Spidergirl. She can practically run up walls. She'd get away from anywhere!"

"It's essential that we interview her," said BB. "If she makes any contact with you, please let me know right away. In the meantime, I'll talk to the relevant authorities and see if the police can locate her."

"Have you spoken to Dr. Freeman?" I asked.

"Not yet—he's currently undergoing a medical and psychological assessment at Holyrood House. The doctor suggests we wait until Dr. Freeman's condition is more stable before we question him. In the meantime, the police and other authorities are trying to discover his identity."

At last the interview was over. As the others stood to leave, I said quietly to BB, "Someone knew D'Merrick was coming. I hope you're working on that too. The only people who knew about her arrival were on our side."

"I know," BB said quietly. His expression was serious as he said goodbye.

2:51 pm

Both Ryan and I needed to spend time with our families and Gabbi had been pestering me to take her sailing and visit Harriet again. I called Winter to ask if we could borrow the keys to

Perdita, her house down the coast.

"I'd come with you," she said, "except I promised Rebecca at the refuge that I'd give her a hand doing some painting."

After we'd agreed to meet for a picnic in a week's time, I said goodbye and headed out of the city for what I liked to think was a well-earned rest.

I tried not to worry about the countdown warning I'd received all those weeks ago. Surely that was all done with now, or being taken care of by SI-6?

But as I continued to count the days off, I wondered what might still be to come.

DAY 70

21 days to go . . .

Harkley's Beach, Dolphin Point

11:15 am

The following week we took Winter's picnic basket down to a nearby beach and spread out a big blanket. It was so good to be back with my friends again. My leg and side were both healing and were not so sensitive now. I'd asked Ryan to join us, but he was hanging out with his mum. She'd been very worried by his absence and was reassured to have him home. He said he'd drop by my place sometime later. I noticed Winter still had paint spots on a couple of her fingernails.

After passing on Harriet's good wishes to Boges and Winter and telling them a bit about the trip I'd made with Gabbi down to Perdita, I told them that I'd heard from Zak and Ariel. "After everything they'd been through on Shadow Island, their mum was over the moon to have them back and they're working things out."

I smiled. "They sounded really happy."

Then I described the debriefing session I'd had with BB, Axel and D'Merrick. I turned to Boges. "How are you doing with cracking that Mordred key?"

"Slow. The word is *slow*," said Boges, grabbing a huge slab of spinach and ricotta pie. "It's so heavily encrypted that Maxine and I are both pulling our hair out over it."

"I'd like to see that," Winter grinned, tousling Boges's thick hair.

"See, what we're looking at isn't any old-fashioned executable system code," Boges said, still flushing from Winter's teasing, "but a really high-level language with sophisticated functionality and direct interfaces . . . with a very strong 1,024-bit RSA encryption key—"

"Hey, Boges," I begged, "plain English?"

"What I'm trying to say is . . . look, it's very complicated," said Boges, crestfallen before he brightened up again. "I've been working really late—"

"Working late with Maxine? Go, Boges!" Winter laughed.

"—working really late on the *Mordred key*," Boges continued in a lofty voice, ignoring Winter's cheeky interruption, "analyzing how it was made, its architecture, any unique modules that it might contain. I just wish we had the capability to crunch numeral data like the Large Hadron Collider."

Boges had told us before about this amazing particle collider built somewhere in Europe to smash atoms in order to prove the existence of a particular particle called the Higgs boson. "Just imagine it, dude! A hundred and seventy computing centers in thirty-six different countries. All trying to prove the existence of this one particle, using this awesome worldwide LHC computing grid. Tens of thousands of computers all working together on one job. If we had that sort of super-computing power, we'd crack this Mordred key easy as!" He clicked his fingers. "But we have to make do with what we've got at SI-6," he said with a sigh as he lay down to digest his lunch in the sunshine.

Just then I heard someone yelling my name and turned around to see Ryan lugging a large rucksack down the beach towards us. I jumped up as he approached and stared at the rucksack. My blood ran cold.

"Hey, guys! Cal, this was just delivered to your place, bro. I was about to knock on your door when a courier van pulled up. I thought it best to bring it straight to you. Know what I mean?"

"You mean keep Mum out of it?" I said.

"You got it!" he laughed.

I took the rucksack and saw that it had a label addressed to me tied tightly to the straps. "This is from Damien, I know it," I said. "This is identical to the rucksacks that I found in the lab—the ones he gave to his Zenith team."

I found myself staring sightlessly at the rucksack as my brain whirred. Then I looked across at Ryan, relaxed and happy, sprawled on the blanket.

Danger—danger—danger went my internal alarm system.

Despite the happy, beachside picnic atmosphere, every instinct was signaling a red alert.

I saw Boges and Winter frown at each other and then stare at me.

"Let's take a look," said Winter, turning her attention to loosening the ties on the straps of the rucksack. As she glanced up at me, my frown remained as the thoughts in my brain started to coalesce. "Cal, what is it?" she asked. "What's wrong?"

On the verge of telling them my fears, I jumped when Ryan's phone rang.

"Hi, Mum," he said. "I'm not far—just down here near the beach with Cal and the others." He squinted against the sun, listening to his mother's voice. "Friends?" he continued, with a puzzled look. "What friends? I wasn't expecting anyone. Who were they? What did they want?"

I realized now that Ryan was in terrible danger. If Damien had organized to deliver this rucksack to me, it meant that he thought he had something to hold over me—or in this case, *someone*. But by sheer good fortune, Ryan hadn't been at home when . . .

Friends. Friends that Ryan wasn't expecting. My red alert was now on fire. I signaled frantically to Ryan and mouthed the words "hang up."

Ryan shrugged and mouthed *OK* as he continued speaking after a pause. "I can be back when they drop by again. I'll come straight home," and hung up. "What's up?" he said, turning to me.

"Ryan," I said, "you can't go home. You're in terrible danger!"

"But Cal, what do you—"

I grabbed his arm. "Don't you see? Those friends—*they weren't friends.* Thoroughgood's already sent people around to your place! It's just dumb luck you weren't at home, otherwise you would have been shoved in somebody's trunk. Don't you see? That's why I've been sent this rucksack—Damien thinks that those 'friends' have already kidnapped you! Except his goons will have alerted him by now that you weren't at home. So now we've got a tiny bit of breathing space while he figures out what to do next!"

"Cal, I don't understand. What's going on?" Winter turned her worried eyes towards mine. Now Ryan was looking scared, his eyes glancing from me to Boges to Winter and then back to me again.

"What did your mum say?" I asked.

"She said two guys from Shadow Island came by to pick me up to go bowling. They said they'd come by later."

"Believe me, they weren't friends," I said.

Ryan got it. He looked at me, eyes wide. His face paled as the awful truth and the lucky escape he'd just had sank in. A slice of pie slid from his fingers. His voice dropped to a whisper as he said, "They were going to use me to force you to do whatever Damien wants, Cal. Just like he tried to do back on the beach at Shadow Island!"

I nodded.

The four of us looked at each other wordlessly. Winter put her arm around Ryan. "We'll keep you safe, Ryan. You'd better stay at my place for a while."

"Or mine, Ryan," said Boges, his thick eyebrows joining together in a worried line. "It might force me to tidy up my room. Last time I tidied it was sometime last year."

I shook my head. "I know a place no one would ever think of checking," I said.

Repro's House
Florence Street, Central

12:58 pm

Repro's place was a tall row house in one of the quieter streets near Central railroad station. There wasn't much conversation among the four of us as Winter drove. We were all thinking the same thing—Damien was coming after me.

Winter pulled over and we got out of the car and went up the couple of steps to the front door. I rapped on it.

"Is he home?" Ryan asked, trying to peer through the frosted glass of the door.

A few moments later we heard someone coming down the hall, grumbling and muttering, then the door opened and Repro, dressed in his familiar green jacket and wearing an extraordinary pair of thick-lensed glasses, blinked magnified eyes at us as he peered out. It was like looking into the face of a giant crazed possum. I'd forgotten Repro's weakness for wearing glasses in the belief that it made him look more intelligent and handsome. Over the years, he'd collected dozens of pairs left on trains by careless commuters.

Before I could explain anything, Repro had launched into a speech, shaking his head to emphasize what he was saying. "It wasn't me," he said. "It might have looked like me, but I can assure you it wasn't me. Whatever it was, I didn't do it because I wasn't there. And even if I was there, it couldn't have been me because I was actually somewhere else when it went missing . . ."

"Repro," I said, interrupting his monologue, "it's me, *Cal*. It's us. If you took off those glasses, you might be able to see who you're talking to."

Repro's voice petered out. He removed the glasses, blinking. "Good heavens! So it is! I thought it might have been something to do with a single-furrow iron plow. It was all rusted and completely useless. And besides, you need a Clydesdale horse to pull one along, and who's got one of those these days? But it had a nice shape to it and I thought it would be a good addition to . . ." He suddenly stopped. "You know I don't like visitors . . . unless there's fish and chips involved."

"We're not here about a plow, Repro. Actually, we've brought you lunch! Now can we come in?"

Repro peered closer, sniffing in suspicion. "What is it?"

"We'll have to come in to show you," I reasoned.

Grumbling, Repro stood back to let us pass

through the narrow hallway. I noticed out of the corner of my eye that both the front rooms we passed were filled almost to the ceiling with Repro's collection—stacks of boxes, old magazines, piles of umbrellas and several towers of hats, all piled on top of each other. Repro muttered, "If you want to sit down, you'll have to find a space somewhere in the living room."

This room still had a little clear space in it. I removed a shop mannequin wearing many layers of dresses leaning against one chair, and the others made room as best they could by shifting piles of paper and a large box full of bright-red suspenders and black bow ties. Ryan settled himself on the floor, pushing an enormous rubber duck into the corner.

We spread out what was left of the spinach and ricotta pie, the container of sliced tomatoes and Winter's fantastic potato salad, and Repro brought out a pile of plates from the coronation of Queen Victoria, together with some blackened silver forks. "I suppose this is all right," he said grudgingly. "I would have preferred fish and chips."

"I know you don't like having house guests," I said, "but this is an emergency."

"On the run again, are you?" Repro said suspiciously.

"Nothing like that. It's Ryan. He needs a safe place to stay while we sort out a more permanent hideout for him."

Repro jabbed some potato salad onto his fork. "Possibly that could be arranged. Maybe the occasional fish and chips dinner would be helpful in organizing such a venture?"

"Done!" I said. "There are some very dangerous people looking for Ryan."

Repro nodded, without any surprise. "I've often been in the same situation myself." He looked around. "Somewhere, there is a very fine, brand-new hospital bed still wrapped in plastic that goes up and down in the most satisfactory way."

I briefly wondered how on earth Repro had acquired a brand-new hospital bed, let alone how he'd managed to get it to his place and in the narrow doorway.

"Ryan, you're welcome to use that," Repro was saying. He frowned, looking around. "That's if you can find it."

"But what can I tell Mum?" Ryan asked, worried. "She's just gotten me back home and now I'm off again."

"I could tell her you're having a sleepover—which is the truth. And she'll probably assume that it's at my place."

"It's just to give us time to come up with a better solution to keep you safe," Winter added.

I slipped my arm around her waist and she gave me a grateful glance.

After the five of us had polished off all the food, Ryan started looking for the hospital bed. He didn't have much luck so I got up to help him. We shifted mountains of clothing and boots until finally Ryan yelled out in excitement. "Here it is, over here! Just as well it's still got its plastic covering on it. Otherwise it would be covered in rust!"

I looked over to see what he meant. On top of the plastic covering of the hospital bed was an old iron plow.

Winter's House
Mansfield Way, Dolphin Point

3:27 pm

Back at Winter's place, I hauled the rucksack up onto the long kitchen counter.

"Are you sure we shouldn't tell SI-6 about the threat to Ryan?" Boges said as I opened the rucksack.

"I'm not confident about telling SI-6 anything more until BB finds out who's been feeding information to Damien," I said. "Ryan's safe for the time being, but he obviously can't stay with Repro indefinitely. In the meantime, let's find out what we've got in here."

I opened the rucksack, carefully pulling out the contents.

"Rations," said Boges, picking up a slab of protein concentrate and a bar of chocolate. "First-aid kit, very safety conscious . . . and what's this?" he asked, lifting out a sealed package, closed with tamper-proof tape. "Should I open it?"

"Of course, Boges," said Winter, taking it from him and tearing it open.

"Hang on," I said. "There are instructions written on the envelope." I read them out loud. "'Do not open until in position and orders received.'"

"You're not going to pay any attention to Damien's instructions, surely?" asked Winter, with derision.

We all crowded around to see what was in the envelope as I spread the contents out on the table. First I saw a computer printout of the details of a one-way plane ticket with British Airways to Heathrow, London. Behind the first page were the details of a second flight from London to Geneva. Beneath that, was a plastic envelope with a passport in it—my passport! There was my photograph and all my personal details. I knew it was a fake, but it was an extremely professional job. With his shady contacts, Damien clearly had access to all types of criminal technology. Also included was a map of an area of Europe—Switzerland, France and parts of Germany. A small red dot marked a place near the Swiss-German border. There didn't seem to be much there.

"Oh," cried Winter, "look down here, that's Lake Geneva. I went there with my parents when I was a really little girl! But that red spot is much closer to the border between France and Germany."

"I don't understand," I said. "Damien didn't mention anything about a place like this. And there was nothing on that map in the lab about another target. This looks like a small town. What am I supposed to do there? All the other targets were major cities."

"What else is in the rucksack?" Boges asked, as I put aside the contents of the sealed package. We pulled out tools, a length of nylon rope, and finally had emptied the whole rucksack.

"That's it," I said.

Boges picked up the rucksack and weighed it in his hands. "It's still very heavy. Either it's an industrial strength rucksack . . . or . . ." He started feeling around the bottom.

"Or what?" Winter asked.

"Or," said Boges, triumphantly diving his hand down into it, ". . . there's a false bottom!"

He pulled out an oval of heavy black plastic, which had seemed to be the base of the rucksack. "Look what's under the false floor! Ta-da! Guess what I've got?"

It was a hologram eye. Boges held it out for us to see. This was the first time I'd been able to see one up close. I took it from him and held it close to my own eyes. It was set in the middle of a square of hard, transparent material, just like novelty holograms in souvenir shops or toy shops.

"It's very disconcerting," said Winter, as I passed it to her, "having one eye glaring at me like this! It looks disgustingly real." She was right. The eye, a gray color, with darker flecks in the iris and a golden ring around the pupil, stared back at me as I examined it. It was unnerving. "What's the story with these eyes?" I asked as the eye was passed around. "What could they possibly be for?"

Of course, nobody could answer.

"Maybe to hypnotize the security guards?" joked Boges, pretending to be a hypnotist. "Look into my eye—my one eye. You are feeling drowsy. Your eyes are getting heavy."

Winter grabbed it from him again. "Look, it's got initials etched on it—just here on the right."

We all peered closer, and sure enough, I could make out the initials *HLH*.

"There's another diagram," said Boges unfolding it and smoothing it out so that we could all look. It was another building plan, yet another unknown target, but this one was different. Instead of the skull and crossbones and the picture of the eye, this one was far more complicated than any of the other diagrams. I couldn't read it clearly at all. It seemed to indicate a number of levels. Maybe this was a very tall building. I tipped up the sealed envelope and shook it, but there was nothing else in it except a strip of paper with a web address.

"Let's log on and take a look," said Winter.

Boges shook his head. "Let's not. If it's an address that Damien is monitoring, he'll know we've accessed it. I don't think we should show our hand just yet."

"What else is in there?" I asked.

Boges felt around again. "Feels like some kids' blocks."

"Careful, Boges. It won't be blocks, it'll be modbots," I said.

"Great! Let's have a look at them!" Boges's face was alive with excitement.

"Be careful! Remember what I told you about the last time I tried to touch one," I warned. "My hand stung for hours."

Boges gently tipped the pile of modbots out

onto the table. They lay there, completely still—no lights, no life at all. Boges cautiously went to pick one up and nothing happened. "They're asleep," he said. "I wonder what switches them on?"

"A signal from somewhere?" Winter asked.

"They're self-organizing," Boges explained. "They don't necessarily need an external signal."

"They moved by themselves in the lab back on Shadow Island," I said, nodding. "So just be careful that they don't switch on right now."

"I really want to have a closer look at one," said Boges, picking up one of the cream-colored cubes, "but I'll need to find out more about them before I do that. I'll talk to my robotic engineer friend."

"You do have a lot of very specialized friends," Winter smiled.

"I try," Boges laughed.

"Maybe I *should* tell SI-6 about this," I said, indicating the rucksack and the modbots.

"I suppose so." Boges sounded very unwilling. "But they'll take everything and I'll never get a chance to have a look at how these modbots work and what they're for."

"My problem is still that until BB finds out who the mole is, I'm not sure if we can trust SI-6 with all this information and the modbots. What if it gets back to Damien?" I said.

"But he already knows that you've got the rucksack," said Winter.

"But I've got it under very different circumstances than he'd planned," I reminded her. "He's got nothing over me now. He'll be furious that I've got the rucksack and can study its contents at leisure, maybe even take it to the authorities, or start working to foil his plan. And he's got nothing!"

"Cal," said Winter, "that just makes him even more dangerous than he was before. He might do something crazy like try to get rid of both you and Ryan, thinking that without your evidence the police have nothing to charge him with. Remember that your whole undercover operation was unofficial—a 'black operation.' SI-6 can't really expose themselves and come to your assistance. We can only rely on ourselves—and each other. We can't expect anyone else to rush in and save us. We have to figure out a way to protect you both from Damien."

We were all silent for a while at her words. Winter was right. We couldn't rely on anybody else to help us.

"OK," I said. "Boges, could you figure out a way to log on to this website without leaving a trace that would alert Damien?"

"I'll make some discreet inquiries. I'm hoping

that the website might clear up a few mysteries, like what this eye is supposed to be for," he said.

"That would be a good start," I said.

"Although," he said slowly, "I'm having a few ideas of my own. But I'll keep them to myself until I'm sure."

"I think you should go and visit Dr. Freeman," Winter said. "He might have remembered a bit more about his past by now."

"Good idea," I said. "I'll check with Holyrood House and find a good time to visit."

"Well, you'd better get going. I need to start working on this web address—and the modbots. That could take some time. Even for a genius like me," Boges laughed.

DAY 81

10 days to go . . .

Holyrood House
Peverill Terrace

2:04 pm

More than a week passed during which we figured out a way to keep Ryan safe from Damien's henchmen. Ryan pretended to be making up for all the worry that he'd caused his mum by spending some of his Ormond inheritance money for them to stay at an exclusive waterfront hotel. He'd also introduced Sophie Bellamy to his mum and the three of them got along very well.

From the description Mrs. Spencer had given us about the two guys who claimed to be friends from Shadow Island, we were fairly certain that one of them was Dean. We had no idea who the other one was. I hoped that in a city of millions of people, Ryan would be hard to track down.

Boges kept working on the rucksack website and the modbots. Because he was such a brain, his science teacher at school had allowed Boges to work on his own "science project" so that he could concentrate on developing his interest in robotic engineering. Winter kept reading up on Arthurian legend, in case there were some clues that might be helpful in cracking the Mordred and Arthur keys.

I had called Holyrood House previously and asked about visiting hours, only to be told that Dr. Freeman was not up to visitors for a while. I tried to wait patiently for the rest of the week, then finally got the green light to visit that weekend.

Holyrood House was a modern private hospital situated in a pleasant Victorian mansion. At reception, I asked to see Dr. Freeman and was directed to a modern building which lay behind the old facade.

Dr. Freeman was sitting in a small lounge with a picture window that looked onto the garden. He turned as I came in and I almost didn't recognize him because he was now clean-shaven and he'd put on weight.

"Cal! Great to see you," he said, jumping out of his seat and coming over.

"How have you been?" I asked, shaking his hand vigorously.

"Much better. I'm talking to a very helpful

psychiatrist. I'm starting to remember a few bits and pieces from my life—like places I've been and people I've met. The doctor's getting me to write down anything that comes to me—anything at all—in case it helps me regain my memory. The police have taken my fingerprints and my DNA, just in case I'm on the medical database." I noticed he had a notepad and pen on the table beside the chair.

"What about that notebook you had on Shadow Island?" I asked, remembering the only possession Dr. Freeman had in his cell on Delta 11.

He frowned. "Notebook?" For a moment, he looked confused. "My notebook! With everything that's happened, I completely forgot about it. I'll ask the hospital. Maybe it was stored somewhere when I arrived."

It was obvious that Dr. Freeman hadn't remembered very much at all so far, so after a few more questions and sharing a cup of hospital coffee with him, I said goodbye, promising I'd visit soon. As he walked to the hallway door with me, he said, "I only hope I can do something one day to show my gratitude to you. Cal, you saved my life."

I made some inquiries at the nurses' station about Dr. Freeman's notebook. "It should have been with him," I said, "when he was admitted." The nurse said he'd look into it and he was sure it would be somewhere safe.

"It's probably been put away for him," the nurse added. "I'll find out."

I thanked him and left, wondering if Dr. Freeman's notebook might have valuable information in it. SI-6 should be informed of its existence. I figured it would be safe to leave a message on BB's personal voicemail. "Please check with Holyrood House regarding Dr. Freeman's notebook. It could be very important."

DAY 85

6 days to go . . .

Boges's House
Dorothy Road, Richmond

12:49 pm

A couple of days later, I had been on the way home after a ride on my motorbike when my phone had rung. Pulling over, I'd seen it was Boges who had called. When I'd called back, he'd sounded excited.

"Come straight to my place," he'd said. "I've got something to show you!"

I'd changed my route to swing past his house. Maybe he wanted to show me one of his new inventions, or there was some new development in discovering how to decode the Mordred key.

Boges met me at the door, his round face beaming with self-satisfaction. "No," he said, in anticipation of my first question, "I haven't cracked the Mordred key, but I've been able to get through to the website disguised as a spammer. Unfortunately, there are more codes within it.

This guy sure likes codes and encryption. But the good news is that I don't think these ones are going to take me very long to figure out. And in the meantime, I've got some more information about Gloria Finlay, Damien's fiancée. Do you remember I told you I'd been spying on Damien's emails to her? Follow me."

I nodded as I followed Boges through the house, waving a greeting to his grandma who was sitting in a chair in front of the television, shelling peas. His mother was just walking in from the backyard with her gardening tools when she saw us coming.

"Hi, Mrs. Michalko," I said.

"You boys look hungry," she said. "Cal, you're too skinny."

"Thanks," I said, "but don't let us interrupt your gardening. I'm fine."

She didn't look convinced, but we continued to Boges's room at the end of the hallway.

His room was looking more and more like the war room underneath the White House—two monitors showed the back and front entrances of their house. Other screens rolled incomprehensible pages of data, piles of cables and computer parts covered all the surfaces apart from his creaky chair and a small cleared area of the desk beside his laptop.

"What's that?" I asked, pointing to the scrolling data on another laptop on the shelf above his desk.

"It's the program I'm running to decrypt the web address from the sealed orders. It could take a little while. The public key was easy, but the private key takes quite a bit longer—like forever. But this is what I really want to show you."

I dropped down onto an old beanbag from where I could watch Boges at the desk.

"So, back to Gloria," Boges continued. "Her email was just too easy to break into and I've tracked down where she's emailing from. It's really strange, because when I googled it, it didn't make sense."

"What do you mean?" I asked.

"Take a look for yourself," Boges replied.

I stared at the satellite photo that Boges had pulled up on his screen. It showed nothing but dense bushland some distance away from the city. Not even one house was visible in the dark forested area.

"She must be in a tree house or something," I said.

Boges grinned. "That's what I thought—for a minute. Then naturally, because I'm brilliant, I took it further."

"Naturally, Boges," I replied.

"I asked about that area when I was talking to Alistair—the guy who's doing the analysis on Biosurge, who, by the way, has almost finished working on it, and he told me all about this new science lab they're getting. And guess what? I discovered that the area is going to be a huge new university science complex, built with a multimillion-dollar government grant. Alistair said it's so new, it doesn't feature on maps yet."

Boges began pacing the room as he spoke. "It's called Science Valley and it's due to open next year. It's nowhere near finished, he said, and only one section has actually been completed because massive drains have had to be built. Apparently some of the land was reclaimed marshland, but they had to leave a lot of the marshes because of the birdlife there. He's not even sure if the water and electricity have been connected yet."

Boges paused, frowning. "So what's this Finlay chick doing out there? Living in the drains?"

"Let's check it out," I said. "Now, who do we know that's good with drains?"

"Dude, I know what you're thinking," Boges said. "We should get Winter, pick him up and do some snooping around on Gloria Finlay."

Science Valley, Morecambe Hill

2:36 pm

"Drains? *Huge* drains, did you say?" Repro asked as we headed out of the city in Winter's car. "And you're looking for a woman called Gloria Finlay?"

"That's right," I said. "I already told you this."

"It's a little-known fact," said Repro, as we turned off the freeway and headed towards the road to Science Valley, "that my grandmother was a Finlay. In fact, her full name was Majella Daniella Madallena de Finlay."

"de Finlay?" Winter queried. "Unusual to have the noble 'de' in front of a Scottish name like Finlay."

Repro was perched in the front passenger seat beside Winter and he twisted around, addressing me and Boges as we sat in the back seat. "Gloria Finlay might be a relation of mine! I've always known I have aristocratic blood."

"Some good drains and a potentially noble relative? Repro, what more could you possibly want?" Winter asked, turning to him with a smile.

"A sausage sandwich, thanks," said Repro, "with plenty of ketchup."

I'd noticed before how Repro took things very literally.

"That might be tricky out here," I said, as

we turned into a very new road with a signpost saying, *Science Valley—1 km.*

Through the trees I could just see a large white building some distance ahead and when we got there, we saw that we were really in the middle of a construction site. I was surprised that there were no people working there. Winter parked her car under a tree and we walked over the dirt to the building.

"This looks like it's going to be the reception area," I said, indicating a lot of footings and trenches that had been dug for further foundations. The wide double doors of the half-completed building were secured with a heavy chain and padlock at which Repro laughed. We were inside in two minutes flat.

"I guess we should stay pretty low-key," I said in a quiet voice, "until we know what's going on here." It seemed deserted and we checked empty offices with no furniture and electrical wiring protruding from holes in the walls and ceilings. Repro swiftly got bored and went back outside to explore the elaborate drains.

I saw him through the large windows of what was going to be a long laboratory, with acres of lab bench space and curved faucets already in position. It was about ten times the size of the lab back on Shadow Island. I watched as

Repro jumped down into the biggest canal and disappeared out of sight. I turned my attention back to the room and noticed that it had a small office attached to it. I looked inside.

This office had a desk and a chair and a waste-paper basket. I looked into the basket and was surprised to find it had been lined with plastic. I looked around and noticed a pen that had rolled onto the floor and an empty paper cup standing on the window sill, half-hidden by the blind. I also saw a square outline in the dust on the desk, laptop-sized. And when I put my eye down close to the surface, I could see the faintest of rings, as if someone had put a coffee mug or cup of tea there.

Then I spotted something underneath the desk, tucked away near the wall. I pulled it out. It was an LED camping light with a solar charger. Someone had been in here at night. But what on earth would Gloria Finlay be doing hanging out here and sending emails? It didn't make any sense at all. As I walked out, I saw Boges looking at me.

"Seen enough?" he asked.

"I'm not sure. Someone's been working in here," I said, showing him the camping light.

"That's a pretty high-powered one, too," he said, examining it. Then he turned his attention to the swivel chair in front of the desk. "Aha!" he said, pinching something between his fingers, saying, "What's this?" and holding it up to me to see.

It was a long, blond hair. Winter appeared at the doorway, alerted by our voices. She walked over and looked at the hair. Then she studied it more closely. "Gloria Finlay?" she asked.

We finished checking out the small office and went back to the main entrance, looking for Repro.

We found him outside, smiling broadly. "Wonderful drains!" he said. "And they'll be even nicer when they're completely covered and built over. Then they'll be all dark and comfy. Did you find anything inside?"

His grin faded to be replaced by a frown as he listened to what we had to say. "But when there's a great big city not too far away, and an unfinished building site out here without any facilities, what sort of person wants to live here?" he asked.

I thought about my time living in drains and sheds, and unfinished building sites. "A person who doesn't want to be found," I said. "For some reason, Gloria Finlay is in hiding."

Boges's House
Dorothy Road, Richmond

5:07 pm

Winter dropped Repro off at home then left us at

Boges's place, saying she needed to go shopping and that she would come by later.

"If Gloria is only using the place at night," said Boges as we walked inside, "that's when we should take a look. Let's pay her a visit tomorrow night."

Mrs. Michalko fussed around us. "I make you some latkes—bring to your room?"

"Thanks," said Boges as we headed to his lair.

"Latkes?" I asked.

"Potato pancakes—pretty good."

My phone rang. "D'Merrick!" I said. "Good to hear from you."

"I thought I'd bring you up-to-date," she said as Boges and I went into his room. "You know how one of our guys recognized one of the diagrams as belonging to the Hong Kong electricity service building? We took a punt that the others might be service offices for the grids of those other cities. That turned out to be the case. As we'd suspected, the diagrams tally with the service office complexes for the electrical grids in Johannesburg, New York, London and Frankfurt."

"He wanted to attack office buildings?" I asked, perplexed.

"Cal, these service centers house the computers that organize the flow of electricity. They are well secured because they could be targeted in a terrorist attack. Interrupting the electricity supply, bringing down the computers that regulate the steady flow, can create absolute chaos in a big city. We've seen it happen in natural disasters. We believe that Damien is planning to do just that. But we don't know how," D'Merrick said. "The security systems at these buildings are state-of-the-art. It's impossible to break into them because they're protected with biometric scanners as well as physical security such as bars and electronically locked doors. At the moment, we have an Interpol alert out for Damien because it's imperative that we find him, otherwise . . ."

D'Merrick sounded concerned. "We're just hoping we can stop him in time. As you know, there's just a few days left until the countdown warning you received finishes—if that's his deadline. From what you've told us, he seems to already have people in position, ready to strike. But unless we can break into that Mordred key, we're in the dark. All we can do is alert these service offices and make sure their security is tight."

"All the Zenith team people were given rucksacks," I said, "with military-style rations and water decontamination tablets. That means . . ."

D'Merrick got it right away. "That means they're camping out somewhere where they'll never be found. I don't know how we're going to track them down. We must find them and we must stop them."

It was time to come clean about the website address in the rucksack and the new diagram. Maybe it too was the service office for an important electrical network. "I have another diagram," I said, thinking quickly. "It must have gotten overlooked before."

"Send it immediately," said D'Merrick, sounding displeased.

Mrs. Michalko interrupted us with a plate of latkes, Winter close behind her.

"I've got to go now, but I'll send that info soon, OK?" I said.

"OK, Cal, please do." D'Merrick hung up.

"Thanks, Ma," said Boges, shooing his mother out of the room. "Don't come in again. It only upsets you."

"Big mess, big mess," protested his mother, as Boges closed the door behind her.

"Yes, yes, I'll clean it up one day. Promise," he muttered with a grimace.

"Last year was the last time," I reminded him.

"Yum," said Winter. "That big pancake's got my name on it!" She took one of the deliciously golden fried latkes from the stack on the plate. "You should call Ryan," she said before taking a big bite.

I grabbed a latke, beating Boges to the next-biggest one. Through my mouthful I said, "We have to let SI-6 in on the sealed orders and the encrypted website. That way they can bring their expertise to the problem." Boges and Winter frowned at each other, pausing in their chewing. Then they both nodded, understanding.

"OK," Boges said, his thick eyebrows raised almost to his hairline. "You'd better tell us all about that conversation."

I did. I repeated what D'Merrick had passed on to me, about the service rooms connected to the electricity delivery systems in the cities where the Zenith team members had been sent.

Boges interrupted me. "They've got to be stopped! I read a report where the FBI did a 'worst-case' exercise, you know, of how things would be if the power for a big city failed completely. It doesn't take long for total chaos. Generators keep things going for a while, but when they run out, there's no way to get fuel, traffic lights don't work, escalators in shops and at railroad stations all stop. The trains stop and people are stranded. Food starts rotting as freezers and refrigerators start to defrost. Fights break out in supermarkets over canned food. The crime rate starts going up as people are robbed and houses are broken into by people getting desperate. And if it takes a while to the repair the system? Bad news . . . I'm talking bows and arrows and there aren't many cats or dogs left."

As Boges spoke, I visualized the sorts of scenes that I'd only seen in movies happening in our streets, in our cities. Winter looked pale. "We've gotta decode that Mordred key," I said.

Boges checked his screen, and then took a closer look. "Dude, we just might be on the way to doing that. My brilliant program has unlocked the coding around the sealed orders."

"Awesome, Boges. Tell me what we've got."

Boges printed out the decoded instructions.

* LOCATION OF PERSONAL DEFENSE SYSTEM WILL BE EMAILED TO YOUR PHONE.

* PICK UP PRIOR TO APPROACHING TARGET.

* APPLICATION OF MORDRED SHOULD BE EFFECTED AS DISCUSSED IN FINAL BRIEFING.

* ONCE MORDRED IS IN PLACE, CALL RELEVANT EMERGENCY SERVICES. USE ONLY THE WORDS FROM THE SCRIPT THAT YOU HAVE LEARNED.

* DECISION TREE: IF THE AUTHORITIES COMPLY WITH YOUR DEMAND, AND ONLY AFTER BANK TRANSFER HAS BEEN CARRIED OUT AND AUTHENTICATED, THEN AND ONLY THEN, SIGNAL ARTHUR.

* IF THE AUTHORITIES REFUSE TO COMPLY WITH YOUR DEMAND, RELEASE MORDRED.

* I WILL BE MONITORING ALL COMMUNICATIONS BETWEEN ALL OPERATIVES. GOOD LUCK.

We read through it again. I was getting a vague idea of Damien's plan. I turned to Boges and Winter. "It's blackmail, isn't it? Whatever Mordred is, it's a threat to the whole system. The operative somehow threatens the system unless the authorities pay up. Is that how you read it, guys?"

"That makes sense," Boges said. "If the authorities pay up, then the Arthur key comes into play and the system is safe—at least for the time being. Blackmailers have a habit of coming back over and over again."

I recalled how the word *Arthur* had unlocked the code that allowed us to get into the submersible. "Arthur somehow undoes things, unlocks things, maybe protects you from Mordred?" I added.

"Right," said Winter slowly, thinking out loud. "So the rightful king—the legitimate king—overthrows Mordred and restores order."

"That's it!" said Boges.

"Not quite," said Winter, looking at me intently, her eyes concerned. "Doing this causes Arthur's death."

"Hey," I said, "let's not take the mythology too far!"

"We really need to find Georgia Montgomery, Cal," Winter continued. "You told us she mentioned the Arthur key. I know you said you weren't sure about her, but she could have more information."

"I wouldn't know how to track her down," I said. "D'Merrick said she disappeared after everyone had landed from the inflatables."

"I've already asked Rebecca at the refuge to keep her ear to the ground. She's promised to call me if she hears anything," Winter said.

"I'd love to know what the personal defense system is that Damien mentions in the briefing orders," I said.

Boges swiveled around in his chair and jumped off it. "Could be something like this. I've created something that might help," he said, "if we get into a tight spot." He went to a drawer and pulled out a small tube. "This is really simple. I've called it Catnap. It's spring-loaded. Much simpler than a syringe. Just press it against a person, press this little button on the end here, and—voila! This tiny needle delivers an immediate knockout punch. Bad guy drops to the floor. I won't try it out on either of you. But believe me, it works like a charm. I practiced on myself and I just dropped like a stone onto the beanbag. I was out like a light for about three minutes. I gave Mum a heart attack when she found me."

"Great," I said. "Wish I'd had that on Shadow Island," I said.

"Dude, you did pretty well without it," Boges laughed.

As I'd promised, I scanned and sent a copy of the multilevel diagram that had accompanied the gear in my rucksack to D'Merrick, hoping that SI-6 would be able to discover what and where this building was.

After talking it over with the others, we also sent through the decoded instructions from the sealed-orders website. The more brains that worked on stopping Damien, the better. As I expected, D'Merrick called me a short while later.

"Thanks for that information, Cal. We're all working on it right now. I'm assuming you don't have any other information that you've forgotten to pass on?"

"No," I replied evenly, sighing to myself as I lied to her. I just couldn't reveal everything about the rucksack—I couldn't risk it with the SI-6 spy still unknown.

"OK, well, Interpol have been given photographs

of the Zenith team members—Paddy managed to get hold of them from Damien's laptop," she said.

"That's pretty impressive," I said, wondering how that could be done remotely.

But I couldn't shake a troubling feeling about that last diagram. It didn't fit the pattern of the others. It was like those picture quizzes we did when we were little kids—spot the one that's different.

That was the sixth diagram—the odd one out.

DAY 87

4 days to go . . .

Science Valley, Morecambe Hill

12:10 am

It was after midnight when we turned off the main
road from the city and onto the track leading
to Science Valley. Winter killed the headlights.
We'd all brought flashlights and I was carrying
my latest little video camera in my backpack.
Slowly, Winter's car tires crunched along the
unpaved road until we were several hundred
yards away from the tall white building, which
we could dimly see by starlight.

"There's bound to be security patrols out
here," I said. "Let's pull off the road and go into
this bushland."

Winter maneuvered the car off the road and
through some dense brush until we were sure
that the car couldn't be seen from the road.
Quietly, closing the doors without any noise, we

got out of the car and made our way through the spiky bottlebrush bushes.

"There's a light over there!" said Winter in a low voice. As soon as she'd spoken, I grabbed her and Boges and pulled them back into the foliage, hissing, "Shh! Don't move!"

Together we peered through the bushes. The light was moving around and it became clear that it was the beam of a flashlight held by a security guard, walking around, checking doors and windows, making sure that there were no intruders. Satisfied, we heard him walking to the left of the building, a car door slamming, and soon after that, the sound of his engine. Within seconds, we watched as a Northern Star Security car bumped down the unpaved road past where we were hiding and onto the main road.

Before the sounds of his car had faded away completely, the three of us were sprinting towards the building.

"Let's check it out thoroughly," I said. "There doesn't seem to be anyone here now, but we might find some other clues."

The padlock on the double doors didn't give us too much trouble—Repro had shown us what to do and even given me a little pick which Winter used very effectively. We were inside quickly, flashlight beams low to the ground, creeping along the corridors we had checked out in daylight less than two days before.

The echoing, empty hallway and unfinished offices seemed eerie in the darkness and only the dimmest of light penetrated from the windows. Even though there was no one to hear us, I kept my voice low when I said, "Let's go to the office where we found the light and other stuff."

By flashlight, I could see that the door to the office was slightly ajar. Cautiously, I pushed it open and stepped inside.

I shrieked in terror as something landed on my head. Fierce claws scratched my head and face. I struggled violently trying to get the terrifying creature off me!

"It's a wildcat or something!" Winter screamed. "I can't grab hold of it!"

"What is it? Hit it with a flashlight!" yelled Boges, swinging his around wildly.

Suddenly, whatever it was dropped to the ground in pieces. Three flashlights shone on it.

Quick as a flash, it reassembled itself.

"*What is that?*" Boges spoke for all of us.

I blinked, forgetting the painful scratches on my forehead and head for a moment. It had reassembled itself just like the spython back on Shadow Island!

Standing on the floor, staring up at us with evil green eyes was what looked like a big black cat. It lashed its tail and bared its teeth at us, hissing, long, sharp fangs gleaming in the flashlight's beam.

"It's not a cat," I said slowly, remembering the snarling metallic dog I'd seen at SI-6's HQ.

"It's a *modcat*, a robocat," Boges breathed in awe, staring in wonder at the green-eyed creature, reaching out to pick it up.

"*Don't touch it!*" I screamed. But my warning came too late.

The black cat reared up on its back legs, metal claws exposed, and swiped at Boges. Four stripes of blood appeared across the top of Boges's hand.

"Yowch!" he yelled as the black cat dropped back onto all fours again. "That really hurt! But you've gotta admit," he added, nursing his badly scratched hand, "that is a pretty amazing piece of work." He studied it by the light of our flashlights.

Now we could see the narrow steel rims around the glaring green eyes, and the fake fur that covered the moving parts. The tail, too, had moved in a somewhat jerky way, rather than waving gracefully like that of a living cat. As we looked at it, its green eyes faded out and it became completely still.

"It's turned itself off," I said. "Just like that robot dog SI-6 used to test me." I was feeling really confused. Was this another test?

"It wouldn't be SI-6," said Boges, voicing my very thoughts, "because that makes no sense at all. But it does suggest someone who can get their hands on very advanced robotics."

I pulled out my video camera and did a quick pan of the office, taking it all in—the desk, which seemed to have a few things scattered on it, but mostly concentrating on the dormant robocat. This time, there was a ceramic coffee cup on the desk. Winter shone her flashlight on it, and touched it. "This coffee cup is still a little warm. You don't think Damien's hiding out here?" she asked.

Before I could answer her, the sound of an approaching car startled us and we switched off our flashlights, scrambling to find a window. The headlights of a car, driving fairly quickly along the unpaved road, shone brightly.

"It must be security coming back again!" I said. "There must be a silent alarm! Quick, let's get out of here!"

We raced to the front door and peered out. The car had parked somewhere out of sight. We ran quickly around the back of the building, trying to see where the car was. Finally we spotted it and the person getting out.

"It's not Northern Star Security," I said, my video camera still running. It was hard in the dim light to see the driver who was now walking towards the front door. I kept filming until the dark figure vanished. "It looked like a woman," I said.

12:33 am

We crept back to our car and Winter kept the headlights off until we were safely on the main road to the city again.

"That was a bit of a waste of time," said Winter, as we cruised back down the highway. I didn't answer her because I was sitting in the back reviewing what I'd shot on the video camera. When I came to the point where the woman got out of the car, I froze the screen and zoomed in, lightening the frame. Boges and Winter were chatting in the front as I stared at the image. The blond hair only covered her ears and part of her forehead. Even though the shadows were deep, the face was one whose features I would recognize anywhere.

I took a deep breath. "Guys," I said, when I'd recovered from the shock and could speak again. "Pull over and take a look at this. We are in very serious trouble."

"What's happened?" asked Winter as she

pulled over onto the shoulder of the freeway.

"Take a look at this!" Winter and Boges looked at the screen as we stepped out of the car.

"I don't believe it!" gasped Winter. "It's not possible!"

Boges words overlapped hers. "Oh no! It's *her!*"

The woman's eyes were hollowed by the poor light, her mouth set in a tight line, her determined face framed by the blond wig. The menacing face glared at us in freeze-frame.

Last time we'd seen her, she was being churned around in a massive surge of water as she was sucked out into the sea when Winter's cellar at Perdita had collapsed into the ocean.

"Oriana de la Force is Damien Thoroughgood's fiancée?" Winter looked at me as if I could somehow change it.

Boges walked around in circles, muttering, "I don't believe it, I don't believe it," as if that would magically remove this deadly woman from our lives.

For a moment, I was speechless too. "Listen, guys. It's no use going nuts about it. We've got to deal with it. It doesn't actually change anything, you know."

"Are you kidding? This is like mixing rat poison with cyanide and getting something a thousand times worse than either of them on their own," Boges cried.

"Come on," I said to my friends. "We can still do this. We've outwitted her before, and this time we've got the advantage because she doesn't know we're on to her. It could be worse."

Boges stopped pacing and looked up from under his eyebrows. "Actually, dude, it *is* worse."

"What do you mean?" I asked, as we got back in the car and took off again.

"That robocat? I'm about one thousand percent sure that those green eyes were camera lenses. Oriana de la Force has almost certainly gotten a good look at us."

I don't think any of us slept very well that night.

Winter's House
Mansfield Way, Dolphin Point

4:25 pm

Later that day, we all met up at Winter's place and replayed my video footage from the night before on her giant plasma television. The big screen revealed details we hadn't noticed before when all our attention had been focused on the robocat. The cat had a little disk around its neck and when we zoomed in on that, we could just make out an inscription—*To Gloria from Damien.*

"Except I bet it's really Jeffrey Thoroughgood's work," Boges said, "and that Damien has just stolen it."

"Don't you think it's a bit odd," I said, as the suspicion started unfolding in my mind, "that SI-6 has such a similar robot dog? Doesn't it seem like there must be some kind of connection?"

"What are you suggesting, Cal?" Winter frowned.

"We know there's a mole in SI-6," I replied, "and this mole has been feeding information to Damien. Maybe I'm overreacting," I said, shaking my head. "Lots of different robotic manufacturers probably make similar products." But I couldn't help feeling that between the two of them, Oriana de la Force and Damien Thoroughgood were capable of almost anything.

We turned our attention back to the video footage and went through it, frame by frame. I concentrated on the desk, examining the coffee cup and what looked like a very expensive fountain pen lying on the desk, next to some handwritten notes.

Winter made a face in frustration. "I could kick myself. I should have twigged that the name Gloria is a shortened version of Gloriana. That was one of the popular names of Queen Elizabeth the first, and we know how obsessed Oriana is with her. She identifies with her."

"She should identify with the black widow spider," said Boges. "That's more her style."

"I'm not sure if knowing about Oriana's part in this earlier would have made much difference," I said. "It just means we have to be twice as clever, twice as cunning, and be prepared to face twice as much danger."

"Great," said Boges. "Just what a guy needs. Double danger."

"Hey, Boges!" said Winter. "There's three of us—four, counting Ryan. Quadruple trouble for those two!"

We were interrupted by the doorbell ringing. Winter went to open it and a moment later Ryan paced into the room. Winter shrugged as she came in behind him. Immediately I knew something was wrong.

"Ryan!" I said, pleased to see him. But his face was angry, and I could tell he wasn't pleased to see me—or any of us. "Hey, what's up?" I asked, standing up to greet him. "Indigestion? Too much luxury living at the resort?" My weak joke fell flat.

"I heard from Repro that you guys went out on a surveillance mission to Science Valley," he said, throwing his jacket over the back of a nearby armchair. "You didn't tell me you were going. Why didn't you include me? Repro said you'd be going out there again. When?"

"Ryan," I said, feeling as if I was confessing to a crime, "I'm sorry, but we've already been."

There was an awkward silence that no one wanted to break. Ryan glared at me, saying nothing. "Look, bro," I tried to explain. "We thought you were having a great time at the resort with your mum—and with Sophie."

"That's not the point! You see me as some sort of problem that has to be solved, just someone to be taken care of, don't you!"

"That's not true. I just didn't think that you'd be—"

"That's the problem, Cal. You just don't think about me—at all."

With that, he stormed out of the room and straight out the front door. Stunned, it took me a moment to come to my senses and I went after him, calling out to him.

"Ryan! Please talk to me," but he kept going until he turned the corner of the street. I ran after him a little way. But then I stopped. It was useless just now. I'd give him time to cool down and then we could talk about it. I rejoined the others back inside. Boges and Winter looked concerned.

"I guess I don't need to explain what just happened," I said. "I've just had so much on my mind. And once I felt he was safe, I didn't think to let him know about what we were doing. I didn't realize he'd be so hurt."

Winter put a hand on my arm. "Don't blame yourself, Cal. Ryan's got his own issues to deal with. I know you two will sort it out."

"Next time we do anything exciting," said Boges, "we'll call Ryan first. I'll remind you, if you forget, OK?"

"It won't do much good," I said, noticing Ryan's jacket still hanging on the back of the chair. "He's left his phone here. He'll be back soon and then we'll sort things out."

My words were interrupted as my phone chimed a text. I didn't recognize the number, but figured out pretty quickly who had sent it.

📱 Hi Cal. Jeremy found my notebook. I've been going through it and the entries and phone numbers are triggering a lot of memories.

I read Dr. Freeman's message to the others.

"At last, some *good* news," said Boges.

DAY 88
3 days to go . . .

Home
Flood Street, Richmond

10:11 am

I'd had a restless night back at home after Winter told me Ryan hadn't been back to pick up his phone. *He must be really angry to cut all three of us off like this.*

I was on a call with Boges when my phone chimed. It was a text message from Winter—

📱 Hang up and call me. Got big news. Wx

"Boges? That was Winter buzzing me. I'll call you right back, OK?" I said. I quickly punched in her number.

"What's up?" I asked.

"Rebecca from the youth center just called. Georgia Montgomery is there and she wants to talk to us."

"Wow, OK. I'll be there in an hour and I'll bring Boges with me," I said.

Bank Street Youth Center

11:23 am

When the three of us arrived at the center, Rebecca motioned to where Georgia was waiting. As we walked into the game room, she swung around from the window to face us, her pointed face set in a determined expression.

"Cal, thanks for coming. I need to talk to you—alone." She gave a pointed stare at Boges and Winter.

"Georgia, these are my best friends, Boges and Winter, and they know about everything that's happened," I assured her. Boges tried one of his winning smiles. Georgia looked unimpressed, but went to the door and looked around before closing it.

"What I have to say is top secret. We have to go through with Damien's plan, Cal. It's the only way to find out what he's up to," she said.

I was about to say that I'd been thinking along these lines myself just in the last few hours, but Georgia continued, "I wasn't the only Zenith team member who ran off. Another guy, Travis, had a fight with Damien back on Shadow Island. Damien had locked him up somewhere, but he managed to escape before the volcano blew up."

A light bulb went off in my head as Damien's

words on the beach came back to me—*One of my champions . . . has become . . . unavailable, and I need a replacement.*

"Travis contacted me once he got to the mainland. He's really sick. I've been taking care of him because he's scared to get treatment in case Damien finds him. That's why I bailed as soon as we got back to shore."

"You should have stayed with D'Merrick and SI-6, they would have taken care of you," I said.

"No way. I'm not trusting anyone at the moment," she said, glaring at Boges and Winter.

"Where is Travis now?" Winter asked gently.

"Staying with some friends," Georgia said. "He's safe there."

"Why don't we go back to my place?" said Winter. "We'll be more comfortable talking there."

"Good idea," I said. "Georgia, maybe we can go over everything you know about Damien's plan again."

Winter's House
Mansfield Way, Dolphin Point

11:58 am

The four of us hunched around the low coffee table in Winter's living room. The surface of the table was littered with copies of the diagrams of the electrical grid service offices in the various capital cities. As Georgia spoke, Boges flipped through the diagrams, frowning.

"We weren't told everything," Georgia was saying in answer to one of my questions. "We had to memorize a lot of things—Damien was paranoid about writing things down. I was supposed to meet Travis in Geneva and wait there without anyone knowing where we were until we received text messages telling us what our target was going to be."

My ears pricked up at the mention of Geneva. Georgia hadn't mentioned that before. How did she know this now? "So what is the target at Geneva?" I asked evenly.

Georgia shook her head. "I don't know. Even Travis didn't know. He was the one who had the weapons."

Boges, Winter and I all exchanged glances. This was the first time we'd heard about *weapons*. But I remembered the close quarters combat training Ryan had talked about on Shadow Island. "What weapons?" I asked.

"Damien developed an aerosol spray using the venom from the stingers. It comes in a tube— looks just like a pen. You spray it on someone's face . . . and that's it. They go down. They'll be out of action for a while."

"That'd be the personal defense system, then," Winter said. Georgia's face was expressionless.

Boges suddenly interrupted our conversation. "Hey, guys? Remember the time we spoofed Oriana de la Force's thumbprint at the bank? I've finally figured out what those hologram eyes are for!"

"Well, tell us!" Winter said.

Boges was interrupted as my phone chimed a text from an unknown number.

We have your brother. If you ever want to see him alive again, you must do exactly as we say. Tell no one. We have eyes everywhere. If you contact the police, we will know. Take your passport and rucksack to the airport. You are booked on the 21:00 flight to London tomorrow night. Carry out the orders you will receive once you are in position or you will never see Ryan again.

I read it again in disbelief as a stab of fear ran through me. I was about to read it out loud to the others when my phone rang. I snatched it up. "Is that you, Thoroughgood?" I demanded angrily.

"It's me, Cal," said Sophie, hurt and startled at my tone. "I hope Ryan's with you. Because he was supposed to meet me today and he hasn't shown up."

The fear tensing my body grew colder and sharper. "Sophie, he's not here." I was about to tell her about the message I'd just received, but I stopped myself in time. Sophie would surely go straight to her father, BB, and report this. I couldn't afford for that to happen. I couldn't risk my brother's life. Instead, I gritted my teeth and feeling like a total loser, I said, "He might be at home, Sophie. You could try calling his mum, Mrs. Spencer? Or he might have just gone off by himself. You know what he's like." I hoped I sounded more convincing to Sophie than I sounded to myself. Boges and Winter were watching me in horror, recognizing the dread on my face.

"OK," she said. "But I was so looking forward to meeting up with him. He said he was going to do some important surveillance work at some place called Science Valley. I'm dying to hear all about it."

As I hung up from Sophie, I looked for Georgia, but she had left the room. The fear in my body had now frozen to ice. "Ryan went to Science Valley—the place that linked Damien and Oriana together. He's walked straight to them."

Boges and Winter stared at me in shocked and stunned horror. Winter snatched my phone from me and read the text message for herself, as if she couldn't believe it and had to see those words with her own eyes.

"What are we going to do?" Boges's words hung in the air as Georgia came back into the room.

"Georgia," I said turning to her, "you must tell us everything you know."

I saw her responding to the desperation in my voice, something softening in her tough little face.

"Cal, I don't know much more than you," she said. "I know there were originally five Zenith teams—pairs of us."

The pages of mysterious names and numbers that I'd found in the folder back in the laboratory at Shadow Island came into my mind. *Zenith one to five. Ten kids, five teams.*

"You said 'originally.' Did something change?"

Georgia glanced at me and I couldn't read her expression. "Damien selected another Zenith team member to take my place, so that I could work with Travis, the elite of the elite champions. We became team six. Damien said we'd have the biggest mission of all. He didn't say much about it because he said we'd be told more once we were in place. Then Travis bolted and you were appointed in his place."

"'Appointed?'" I said, angry. "Hardly! I'm being *forced* into it. I have to do what Damien says if I want to see my brother again. There was another name and list of numbers," I recalled. "Melehan 1, Melehan 2, and so on. Do you know what they are?"

"Those numbers are the identifiers of each module of the modbots. There are ten in each set and each has different capabilities. We all got a set. Have a look at the ones in your rucksack."

I pulled out two modbot segments. Both were dormant, but I handled them cautiously, ready for anything.

"Turn them over and you'll see what I mean."

I gingerly turned over each modbot cube and sure enough, in minute letters, I was just able to read a tiny imprint on each of them.

"These are Melehan 4 and Melehan 5," I said. "I wonder what they do?"

"I can't remember, but I guess all the other Zenith team kids had the same thing," Georgia said. "I'd better be going now. I've got stuff to pick up from the refuge." And with that, she abruptly said goodbye.

"That is one odd girl," Boges said as the front door closed.

"Maybe she's just messed up from everything that happened on the island," Winter offered.

"Maybe she's just odd," Boges replied.

I kept trying to make sense of what she'd said. She seemed to know a lot more than she'd let on when we were on Shadow Island. My thoughts were interrupted by my phone. I snatched it up. This time the text was very short.

📱 Are you prepared to carry out my instructions? Yes or no?

It was a no-brainer. Even while my desperate mind was searching for a solution to this impossible situation, my fingers had already pressed the letters for "Yes" and sent them back to my enemy. I looked up at the others and saw my own shock and fear mirrored in their faces. "I've gotta go through with it," I said. "There's no alternative."

"But what if Damien doesn't keep his side of the bargain?" Boges finally asked. "What if you do what he wants . . . and . . . and . . ."

"—and we never get Ryan back?" Winter finished the terrible question.

"We've gotta tell SI-6," said Boges.

"No way, Boges!" Winter cried. "What if Damien's spy tells him Cal has contacted SI-6? Then Ryan might be in terrible danger. No, Cal has to play along while we try to figure out where he's holding Ryan."

I buried my face in my hands. The situation was impossible. "Winter, Ryan's life is at stake! We can't do both!" I said, my voice cracking.

"But Mrs. Spencer will contact the police if Ryan is missing too much longer," Boges said. "And what about *your* mum as well? Suddenly you two go missing—everyone will notice! The police will be out looking for you, SI-6 will be looking for you both."

"OK, so we have to come up with something that will cover up both of you being MIA," Winter said.

I remembered Dad's slogan from when he was caught in a war zone doing a story years ago— keep calm and carry on. As my mind cleared a little, I thought of a way to cover our absence. I grabbed a piece of paper from Winter and wrote a quick note for my mother.

Hi Mum,
   Ryan and I want to go backpacking together, just for a little while. We figure it'll be good for us to reconnect again. Funnily enough, I wasn't able to spend much time with him on Shadow Island because we were in different groups.
   We'll keep in touch of course.
                    Hugs to Gabbi,
                    Cal and Ryan

Then I grabbed Ryan's jacket and pulled his phone out, quickly texting his mother.

📱 Hi Mum, Cal and I are taking off for a few days to go backpacking. We're still learning how to be brothers to each other. Hope that's OK. Love Ryan.

It was the best I could do with my heart and my head going crazy about Ryan. I had no illusions about what Damien was capable of. I knew he was a ruthless man, who would have no hesitation in eliminating any threat or obstacle that got in his way.

"That should keep the mothers happy for a while," I muttered. "Until I bring Ryan back."

Winter squeezed my hand. "We can do it, Cal. I know we can."

I'd never wished more that she was right.

DAY 89

2 days to go . . .

Winter's House
Mansfield Way, Dolphin Point

4:14 pm

Winter and Boges helped me get my gear together. I'd been booked on the nine o'clock flight to London with a connecting flight to Geneva the following day. The nightmare was real and I was in it.

All the while, my fear about Ryan ran like a black underground river. Now, all I could do was wait and the waiting was like a toothache—painful and all-encompassing.

Boges worked feverishly at his laptop, running program after program, desperately trying to get past the Mordred key's impossible encryption. Winter walked across the room and back again, unable to be still, staring sightlessly out through the open windows, occasionally pausing to put an arm around my shoulders, before continuing with her tiger-like pacing. The low coffee table was covered in piles of paper and notes, copies of the diagrams that we'd made, hoping to get more understanding about the unknown building plan which had come in my rucksack. It stood packed and waiting, near the front door.

Ryan's phone rang and I snatched it up, stupidly and hopelessly thinking it might be him at the other end. Instead, I found a text message from Sophie Bellamy. I read it aloud to the others.

📱 Good news. Johannesburg Zenith team member picked up, singing like a bird says Dad. But she got sick and had to go to the hospital. Hoping to pick up others soon. Interpol working very hard to locate operatives near Frankfurt, London and New York. How come you left without saying goodbye?

She'd signed off with a sad face and a couple of kisses.

I texted back.

📱 I'm sorry :(Promise I'll make it up to you when I get back. Great news about arrested Zenith girl. Hope all rounded up soon. xox Ryan.

5:09 pm

"We'd better go," said Winter, gathering up her own notes and looking around for her jacket and bag. I went to close the window and took a last look at Winter's front garden which was blooming beautifully.

A strange sound caught my attention. Something was buzzing, like a bee. I looked up and saw a small airplane, its wingspan no bigger than my arm. It was flying fast towards Winter's place. "Hey, Boges," I said, "have you got something fancy up in the sky around here? Like a spy plane?"

Boges barely had time to answer. With a burst of speed the small craft came rushing out of the sky straight towards me! Instinctively, I ducked, at the same time yelling to the others, "Get down! Get down!"

I heard them drop to the floor without hesitation and I did the same. Could this plane be delivering something dangerous, something to harm us? But why would my enemies be trying to kill me before I even got to London? I covered my head as best I could, peering out of the corner of my eye. The small plane flew in the window and around the room, dropped something on the table and then flew out of the window again. Stunned, I slowly climbed to my feet.

"What was that all about?" asked Boges, racing to one of the windows and staring up into the sky.

"Whatever it was," Winter answered, looking out the other window, "it's gone."

Cautiously, I went to the table. A small black envelope lay crookedly on top of piles of paper. It carried the logo of the world map with the skull and crossbones.

"From Damien," I said, cautiously picking it up. "There's something inside." I opened the envelope as if it contained a funnel-web spider, tipping it upside down.

Out fell a heavy, complicated-looking security key and a small square of cardboard—

As if I could forget, I thought bitterly, staring at the underlined words.

"We don't even have time to find out anything about it, which is exactly how Damien planned it, of course," Winter added angrily.

"And he's been watching me this whole time," I said. "He knew I was here with you guys rather than at home."

"He'll have someone watching you on the flights, too," said Winter.

Of course he would, I realized.

City Airport, International Departures

8:02 pm

It was hard saying goodbye to my friends.

"I feel like I've failed you, dude," Boges said, as he gave me a final hug. "I thought I'd have that Mordred encryption opened up for you so you'd know what you were up against. Maxine and I will work around the clock on it, I promise."

"You've never failed me, Boges. Don't talk like that," I said.

Winter threw her arms around me and hugged me so hard I could scarcely breathe.

"Hey," I said, "take it easy. I'll be back before you know it."

She turned those eyes on me. "You'd better." It sounded like a threat. Then she threw her arms around me again.

Finally it was time to walk past the point of no return. I looked back and gave them one last wave. I could see that Winter was holding back tears. She'd tried her best to smile. It hadn't worked. Boges just looked wretched.

At Security, I lifted my rucksack onto the moving conveyor belt and as it went through the machine to be checked, the conveyor belt stopped. A security guard took me aside so that he could witness me opening my rucksack on a nearby table. He asked me to take out the modbots and I did, lining them up like a little train.

"What are these?" he asked.

The modbots lay completely dormant in a line along the table. Nothing like the truth, I thought.

"They're modbots," I explained. "Modular robots."

"What do you do with them?"

"I don't do anything with them. They're kind of an experiment."

The security guard picked one up and I prayed that it wouldn't switch itself on and sting him or spray him. That would be disastrous—for me and for Ryan.

Now the guard was squinting into the narrow, symmetrically spaced apertures, where the harpoons had come out and jabbed my hand. "What goes on in there?" he asked.

Please, modbots, don't do anything.

"They can be attached to each other," I said,

trying to hide my anxiety and nervousness in case he thought I looked guilty.

"How so?" he asked suspiciously.

"They're building blocks," I said. "Little robot blocks."

"Some kind of novelty?" he suggested, relaxing a little. But then he pulled out the hologram eye in its transparent casing. "What is this?" he asked, holding it up.

"School project," I said quickly. "Biology assignment."

"Boy, you must go to a weird school!" he said, shaking his head.

I was only too happy to go along with that. Finally he waved me through and watched me carefully as I packed up my rucksack again.

I was just moving through into the airport lounge, relieved that I'd gotten past that hurdle, when my phone went.

"Dude! The eye—the eye! I completely forgot to tell you!" Boges's voice was high with excitement. "Remember when we faked Oriana's thumbprint? At her bank?"

"Huh?" I asked, wondering why on earth he was talking about that again now.

"Biometric scanning," said Boges. "Think about it. The hologram eyes are spoof eyes! They've been made to fool the security scanners at the Zenith targets!"

My jaw dropped. "Of course!"

"I was about to tell you yesterday," said Boges, "but with everything that happened, it slipped my mind. That's what the eye symbol means on those diagrams—that's where the biometric scanner must be positioned in each of those buildings. It scans the iris of anyone wanting to come into the building and lets them in if it recognizes them."

"That explains why they were different colors," I said. "They must belong to important people who work in those buildings—the boss, or the head of security or someone." I thought for a moment. "So you reckon all I need to do," I said, frowning, determined to get this right, "is hold the eye up to the biometric scanner when I get there? Wherever 'there' is."

"That's my theory," said Boges. "You're the one who'll be testing it."

DAY 90

1 day to go . . .

Heathrow Airport, London

12:11 pm

I had dozed through most of the flight to London. It was the only way I could get a little relief from my fears about Ryan, by zonking out for a while in restless sleep as the long day finally came to an end. But I'd kept waking up with a jolt and then the horrifying reality would hit again—my brother was in the hands of Damien Thoroughgood, and I was about to carry out some terrible crime on his behalf.

Whenever I was awake, I'd walked up and down the aisles of the airplane, getting a bit of exercise as well as trying to scope out whoever might be a spy operating for Damien. It could have been anyone. A sweet little old lady in a purple beret had watched me with keen, sharp eyes. *Is it you?* I wondered.

I had a three-hour wait at Heathrow before

the flight to Geneva. The minute I switched my phone back on in the airport lounge, there were texts from both Winter and Boges.

📱 Hope you had a good flight. Boges and Miss Brilliance very excited. They've cracked Mordred. Don't give up hope! Wx

I texted back.

📱 Great news! No surprises here so far.

Then Boges's message.

📱 Mordred decoded. Dancing on table!

I replied.

📱 Great! WHAT DOES IT MEAN?

📱 We're working on that!

I tried getting excited about this news, but thoughts of Ryan intruded. There was a slim chance that cracking Mordred might somehow lead to Damien and then my brother might be freed, but all I could think of was Ryan, alone and scared, and me unable to help him. I recognized quite a few people from the earlier flight who were also traveling on to Geneva, including the lady in the purple beret. Another guy stood out—a mean-looking man in his thirties, wearing a ponytail, a black jacket and carrying a rucksack a bit like mine. But he could have been a hiker in a bad mood. My paranoia was making everyone a suspect.

I kept an eye on him as we stood in line at the security checkpoint, prior to boarding the airplane. I still had no idea what I was going to do when I got there. All I could do was wait for instructions.

Geneva International Airport

7:16 pm

We landed at the Geneva airport a few hours later. I followed the signs, hearing many different languages spoken around me, and pulled a heavier jacket out of my rucksack. I'd noticed the chill in the air as we disembarked from the airplane. This was summer?

As I was putting it on, my phone chimed a text. It was Boges.

📱 Bad news dude. Only cracked the outer encryption. More encryption within. Looks like Mordred is a super virus. Don't know what it does but could be bigger and badder than Stuxnet.

My heart sank. I remembered Boges telling me once that Stuxnet was a computer worm—a type of computer virus that had partially destroyed the Iranian nuclear weapons program. And Boges was using Mordred in the same sentence. This was getting worse and we were getting nowhere. I had to stop believing there would be some eleventh-hour breakthrough to save me from carrying out Damien's orders.

I slipped my phone back into the pocket of my big coat and it chimed again almost immediately.

An unknown number.

▯ Take train to city center.

Paranoid, I tried again to pick who it was that seemed to know my every move. But in all the people milling around heading for either the French or Swiss border control lines, it was impossible to single out any individual who looked as if they might be on Damien Thorough-good's payroll. To me, they all looked suspicious now.

I looked around and saw an information desk where I discovered I could get on the shuttle train for free. The information desk had racks of travel brochures, advertizing the local museums, galleries and other attractions. I had ten minutes before the next train so to distract myself from anxiety, I flicked through some of the English-language ones.

A brochure about the largest machine in the world, the Large Hadron Collider, caught my attention. Boges had been talking about it only recently. It was a massive scientific instrument, connected to the most powerful supercomputer system in the world, specially built to study the smallest known particles by smashing them together at the speed of light. It suddenly dawned on me that the collider was right here, somewhere very close to Geneva. I started reading.

LARGE HADRON COLLIDER

Physicists at CERN, the European Council for Nuclear Research, hope to recreate the conditions at the birth of the universe just after the Big Bang in the Large Hadron Collider,

or LHC. Scientists have built a seventeen-mile underground installation containing a massive tube through which particles traveling in opposite directions collide. This tube runs through a huge man-made tunnel passing under several countries at a depth of a hundred yards. When the particles collide head on at the speed of light, their destruction produces even smaller particles. This data is recorded by thousands of scientists from all over the world using tens of thousands of computers to analyze the results.

Boges had lamented that he and Maxine Flint didn't have access to something like this.

Some of the scientific information in the brochure was a bit beyond me, and so I turned my attention back to information about the experiments being carried out at the LHC. Their names were weird acronyms—names made out of the initials of their full names. Four of them—ATLAS, CMS, ALICE and LHCB—were located in huge underground caverns at different points around the tunnel of the collider, a bit like enormous underground railroad stations. The other two smaller experiments didn't have stations of their own but were attached to two of the bigger ones. I was just about to put the brochure back in its stand when I noticed the last sentence. I stared at it, my heart beginning to pound.

"'The seventh experiment, SKALD,'" I whispered to myself, "never got beyond start-up. It required massive amounts of power, and for safety reasons, was reluctantly closed down.'"

SKALD—the seventh experiment!

Damien had talked about a seventh experiment. Was he referring to SKALD? Or was it just a coincidence? I racked my brains trying to think exactly what he'd said. My thoughts were interrupted by the arrival of the train so I shoved the brochure into my pocket and climbed on board.

Genève-Cornavin Station, Central Geneva

7:37 pm

The ride took just over five minutes, and then the train slowed and stopped at the station in the middle of Geneva. Hauling my rucksack, I walked out of the station into the beginnings of twilight and the cool early evening air. It was summer here, but it sure didn't feel like a summer night back home. The wet streets gleamed with the reflected lights from eateries and shops, and traffic slowly heaved along, the occasional horn blaring in the distance.

I texted Boges.

▌ Find out everything you can about SKALD—aka the seventh experiment at the LHC.

I sensed someone following me and looked behind to see someone duck into a doorway. I hurried back and looked in through the window of the crowded cafe. I scanned the faces inside anxiously—would I spot the man with the ponytail or the woman with the purple beret? Or was my imagination making my paranoid? *Snap out of it, Cal!*

My phone chimed, making me jump. I hoped for good news about the Mordred file from Boges, but a wave of fear went through me instead as I read the text.

📱 Wait outside Notre Dame cathedral.

Where was that? I looked around and it didn't take me long to spot it—an ornate, gothic sandstone building, with a statue perched over the large doorway. I crossed over the road and stood on the bottom step outside the church, waiting—waiting for what?

I was glad of my thick coat, as the temperature began to drop with the setting sun. My phone buzzed in my hand. I braced myself as I opened the message. This time there was no text. Just a photograph—a hunched figure on a low stool in almost darkness, bowed over with his head in his hands. It was Ryan, handcuffs on his wrists. Above him, on the grimy wall, I could see a digital clock counting down. It showed four hours and twenty-three minutes left. I closed my eyes, recoiling from the thought of Ryan trapped under this countdown. Another message came through.

📱 This is all the time Ryan has left until he meets Grendel.

I gritted my teeth against the rage that now arose in me. *Who was Grendel?* As I studied the photo, staring at the miserable figure of my brother, I vowed again that I would make Damien pay for this.

That's why I didn't hear them as they came up behind me.

Too late I tried to fight back, but I was over-powered before I could make a sound and hauled backward, my phone flying from my hand.

"Let me go!" I yelled, but a large hand was clamped over my mouth and I was dragged then pushed towards the open door of a waiting car.

Struggling, I tried to get out, but I scarcely had time to glimpse the men sitting in the car before something was shoved over my head and what felt like a kick to my back sent me sprawling onto the seat inside. "My phone!" I cried. "I've gotta get my phone!"

"Be quiet!" a thickly accented voice commanded. "You won't need it where you're going." My ruck-sack was thrown roughly next to me as the car screeched away, leaving my phone on the street. I knew then I was really on my own.

"Who are you? What's going on?" I persisted, while my body was being flung around as the car navigated the city streets.

"Shut up and do what you're told!" came the cold voice again.

I sat there, rigid, squashed between two men in the back with the driver in front, listening to them murmuring together in German. Not knowing what they were saying made my situation even more frightening. But the thought of Ryan in the hands of Damien helped me summon up my courage. I would simply have to face the consequences of carrying out Damien's commands and if that meant going to prison, that was a consequence I would have to accept. Ryan's safety was my first priority—my only priority.

UnKnown Location

10:03 pm

I don't know how long we drove for because time seemed distorted as I tried not to suffocate under the hood. Finally I'd sensed the car slowing down and stopping.

"Get out," said a rough voice close to my ear and I heard him unlock the car door, step out and pull me after him. He took the bag off my head, dropped my rucksack to the ground and as I looked around the dark night outside, he gave me a push.

"Pick up your rucksack and walk!"

I was in the middle of nowhere. Dark, dripping trees surrounded me and all I could see was dense forest, the sky only slightly paler with no stars or moon.

"Walk where?" I asked, looking around.

With another rough push he barked, "Through the gates, *dummkopf!*"

I didn't have to know what dummkopf meant to know it wasn't friendly.

Within moments, he'd jumped back into the car which took off, leaving me stranded in the middle of what appeared to be a black forest of swaying trees.

Gates? What gates? I thought, desperately looking around at my surroundings. Gradually, things came into focus. There *were* gates some distance away—huge, iron ones—almost invisible among the shadows and the winding vines that grew all over them. They were attached to a high stone wall, with weeds growing out of the cracks in the mortar.

I stumbled towards them, wishing I had my phone or a flashlight. The gates were padlocked together. How was I supposed to get in? I pulled out the key that I had safely secured in my zippered pocket and tried it. No luck—this key was for a completely different lock. My eyes were well-adjusted to the darkness by now and I spotted an overgrown path leading towards the dark, unlit building set back from the gates. I looked around for a way in. Surely on a neglected property like this, there'd be some weakness I could exploit.

I started making my way around the wall

through tangles of blackberry bushes which tore at my clothes.

Beyond the trees and thorn bushes, I could see what looked like an old building. Finally I found a section of the wall where I could climb over. I pulled myself up and swung a leg over. A deep growl startled me. Then the growling broke into a snarling bark. I looked down straight into the jaws of a huge German shepherd dancing beneath me on the other side of the wall. This would be the moment to put Plan B into action. *Except I still don't have a Plan B.*

I started clawing my way along the top of the stone wall, but the dog followed every move I made, shadowing me along the ground, several feet below. *Think, Cal, think,* I told myself. From up here, I could see an official-looking sign and could just make out the big letters.

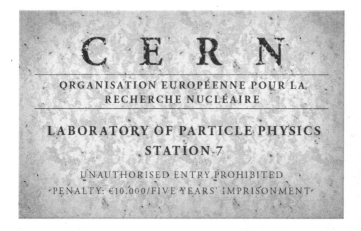

CERN

ORGANISATION EUROPÉENNE POUR LA
RECHERCHE NUCLÉAIRE

LABORATORY OF PARTICLE PHYSICS
STATION 7

UNAUTHORISED ENTRY PROHIBITED
PENALTY: €10,000/FIVE YEARS' IMPRISONMENT

I was right! The seventh experiment Damien had mentioned was the one CERN shut down years before. What had we gotten ourselves into?

I looked closer at the building. It just looked like any other industrial estate and appeared completely deserted. In a shadowy alcove at the front, I could make out recessed metal doors. Beneath me, the dog continued its vicious barking and jumped up on its back legs to snarl at me. Deserted, but not unguarded, it seemed.

I swung around at a noise behind me. "Who's there?" I called out. I stared into the darkness of the forest, certain I'd heard something.

A figure flew out of the dark and before I had the chance to react, he'd pulled himself up onto the wall beside me. I pushed myself back, putting distance between us. Beneath us, the German shepherd was going crazy.

"Who are you and what do you want?" I shouted. I leaned forward, wrenching the hoodie back from his face so I could get a good look at him. Except he wasn't a him!

"*Georgia?*" I blinked, stunned. "What are you doing here?"

"Trying to get over this wall, if you really want to know," she said. "That dog looks very serious! You could let me go now, Cal. I just wanted to surprise you."

"Well, mission accomplished!" I said sarcastically, letting go of my grip. "But how did you get here? How did you know I'd be here? And where did you get that rucksack?"

"After you left, Winter and Boges told me about you coming to Geneva and so I got a flight right away. The rucksack was delivered to the youth center so I thought I'd better come and help you." I wondered for a moment about why my friends might have contacted Georgia.

"But how did you know I'd be *here*—sitting on this stone wall? Right now?"

"Because I knew about the seventh station," she said. "I'd overheard Damien talking about it on the phone to his girlfriend. He said they could visit it together—afterwards."

"After what?" I asked.

"He said he could buy her anything *afterwards*. He thought that was a great joke—but I didn't get it."

Maybe he was talking about the castle in Scotland that he'd promised to buy her as a wedding present. More than likely Damien was just stringing Oriana along. My bet was that he was just using her in the same way that he used everybody else. And she'd be using him, too, I knew, remembering the sort of person she was. They really deserved each other.

I turned my attention back to Georgia, who was looking at me expectantly. "Well?" she asked. "How are we going to get in there?"

"We?" I said pointedly, but Georgia just smiled. I was pretty sure now that I couldn't trust this girl as far as I could throw her. But if I was going to have someone here with me, Georgia wasn't a bad option. I knew how gifted she was and her talents might come in handy.

"Nice doggie," Georgia was saying. The German shepherd seemed to disagree. It continued to run backward and forward just beneath us, snarling and growling.

"OK, here's the plan," I said, as one formulated in my mind. "You go down to the other end of the wall—" I pointed to the right "—and act as if you're about to jump down. While the dog is down there trying to get you, I'm going to make a dash for those double doors over there."

"Then what?" Georgia asked quizzically.

"While the dog's coming after me, you jump down. That way we're both inside," I said.

"What about the dog?"

"I'll think of something, OK?"

Georgia didn't look convinced. "I guess . . ."

Georgia deftly scrambled to the other end of the wall. "Hey, doggie! I'm going over this wall, OK?"

The German shepherd raced up to the other end of the wall where Georgia was leaning over and they traded insults with each other.

I jumped down and raced across the cleared area past the sign prohibiting unauthorized entry and into the darker recess where the double doors loomed.

I tried the key from my pocket. Nothing happened when I turned it. My plan was not working. Behind me, I could hear the dog going crazy and when I turned around, Georgia was no longer to be seen. What if she was on the ground and the dog was savaging her? I raced over, almost tripping on bits of rock strewn around. No Georgia. No dog. But I could hear it barking around the side of the building. What was going on?

"Hey, Cal! Up here!" I looked up and there was Georgia Montgomery on the flat roof of the building not far from the entrance. "You'd better grab my hand quick!"

I could hear the dog coming, its frenzied barking getting louder by the second. I grabbed Georgia's hand as she lay on the roof and extended her arm. Weighed down by my rucksack, I managed to haul myself up onto the roof with her help. Below us, the dog snapped its jaws in frustration.

"How did you do that?" I asked with admiration.

"I kept going around the fence and there was

a tree—I did one of my Spidergirl jumps. From the fence to the tree, from the tree to the roof. It wasn't that far. And here I am."

"What now?" I asked.

"You mightn't have found this," she said, "if I hadn't been here to show you."

I leaned over to see what she was talking about. Just beneath us, a little lower than the underside of the roof, a small metal housing protruded from the masonry.

"It's the scanner," Georgia was saying. "You've got an eye in your rucksack?"

She was right. To anyone approaching the entrance at ground level, the scanner would have been just to the right of the doors at about head height.

I dug around in the rucksack until I found the eye in its compartment. I guessed whoever HLH was, he or she must have had clearance to get into this building. I hoped Damien had done his research thoroughly.

"Hold the eye near the scanner and see what happens," Georgia said.

I leaned down from the flat rooftop, holding the hologram eye right in front of the scanning camera while the dog jumped around going crazy.

As I did, I heard a beep, then a small but definite "click." The double doors trembled as an electronic lock released inside. Miraculously, this unexpected metallic sound spooked the dog! It jumped backward snarling with its tail between its legs.

"Quick! Jump down while we can!" I hissed, and jumped. I landed heavily just next to the doors and as the dog came for me, I heard Georgia thud down behind me and race through the open doorway.

As the dog charged, I banged it over the head with my rucksack which gave me just enough time to dive inside. The doors were already closing. Georgia stood with her hand on the "Close Doors" button just inside the entrance.

Outside, the dog hurled itself at the closing gap, but it was too late. We heard it whimpering outside, claws scraping against the steel.

CERN, Station 7
Swiss-German Border

10:29 pm

I looked around as my heart rate fought to return to normal. A downlight had switched on and I could see that we were in a small, square foyer and ahead of us was a sheer wall of steel, running floor to ceiling. I looked it up and down. It was impenetrable. Station 7 was proving to be very difficult to get into.

"Look! There's another lock here!" Georgia cried, pointing to a small square on the right-hand side of the steel wall.

"And I've got a key," I said, again taking out the key that had been delivered to me yesterday by one of Damien's drones. *Wow, was that just yesterday? It feels like a lifetime ago already.*

Hesitating only for a moment, I pushed the key home. It fit perfectly and I turned it to the right.

Thunk! Thunk!

Invisible bolts thudded back, unlocking the steel wall and pulling it upward like a garage door, revealing what looked like a huge industrial or factory workshop. In front of our surprised eyes, lights blinked on in brilliant rows along banks of computers and monitor screens visible along a long lab bench nearby. Machinery started humming as a huge freight elevator rose from somewhere in the depths underneath us. It stopped on the ground level and opened its doors.

I stared all around me in disbelief! Though it might appear to be crumbling on the outside, this old building actually housed a state-of-the-art industrial engineering site. The bank of computers started running data on their screens. A banner of running green lights swirled around the walls spelling out the same phrase over and over again:

SYNTHETIC HAON ACCELERATION AND LOSS DETECTOR ACTIVATED
SYNTHETIC HAON ACCELERATION AND LOSS DETECTOR ACTIVATED
SYNTHETIC HAON ACCELERATION AND LOSS DETECTOR ACTIVATED
SYNTHETIC HAON ACCELERATION AND LOSS DETECTOR ACTIVATED
SYNTHETIC HAON ACCELERATION AND LOSS DETECTOR ACTIVATED
SYNTHETIC HAON ACCELERATION AND LOSS DETECTOR ACTIVATED
SYNTHETIC HAON ACCELERATION AND LOSS DETECTOR ACTIVATED
SYNTHETIC HAON ACCELERATION AND LOSS DETECTOR ACTIVATED

SKALD—the seventh experiment! But what was I supposed to be *doing* here? SKALD had been closed down because it was too dangerous to run. But from what I could see in front of me, SKALD was now up and running! Is that what Damien wanted me to do? In my ignorance, turn the key and switch on this dangerous seventh experiment? What would happen next?

"I can hear people coming. Quick! Let's get into the elevator!" Georgia whispered.

We ran to the elevator and jumped in, the doors closing automatically. It must have sensed us getting in. Immediately, the elevator started moving downward.

The elevator descended slowly through a shaft cut through rock. It seemed to take forever until finally the cage stopped, the doors opened and we stepped out, looking around us in fascinated fear.

We were standing on a cement platform in a space that reminded me of a gigantic underground train station, but about ten times bigger. And in the hollow tunnel where a train might have traveled, instead there was a massive tube that ran out of sight in both directions. I pulled the brochure out of my jacket and opened it at a picture taken of a section of the Hadron Collider. This was it! This was the huge tube that the particles raced around in! We were standing in one of the enormous bays, hewn out of rock, which housed the instruments physicists used to gather data from their experiments.

Running up and across the massive tube, like a pedestrian bridge over a roadway, was a steel platform with access steps up to a landing. There sat a line of six computers. As I watched, the six monitors flashed into life as the computers booted up. It suddenly hit me that this was the base station for the SKALD experiment—the seventh experiment—housed right here next to the massive circuit of the collider. It was considered too dangerous to start up and *I'd just switched it on!*

10:34 pm

A loud Klaxon, like the worst sort of car alarm, started blaring its staccato warning through the echoing cavern. Red warning lights flashed as a large screen, together with a running digital clock, lit up. My eyes quickly scanned the message:

CAUTION—OVERLOAD WARNING! EMERGENCY
SHUTDOWN WITHIN 10 MINUTES!

Now, over the howling of the alarm, I could
hear someone calling from way up the tunnel.
"Hey! Is anyone down here? What's going on?"

Off in the distance, I saw the small figure of
a guy riding a Segway, heading in our direction.
Georgia grabbed my arm.

"Cal! We have to hide!" she said.

To our right was a door marked *Distribution
Center.* The door was ajar.

"Quick! In here!" she cried and together we
raced into the room. I pushed the door shut. I
heard the thud as the lock engaged. I tried the
handle. It didn't budge. It had automatically
locked from the outside. *Now what?*

At least this gave me a little time to think
of what to do next. I took a deep breath and
examined our surroundings. It seemed to be some
kind of service room with a collection of orange
cabinets, each with a country's name on the front,
and another bank of computers and monitor
screens above running incomprehensible data. I
read the names on the cabinets—*Italy*, *France*,
Germany, *Switzerland* . . . and was puzzled
for a moment until I read some small print on
the wall and realized that the cabinets housed

electrical distribution lines and above them, computers monitored and governed the electrical supply coming from these countries. The SKALD experiment must have been connected to these European nations.

Outside, the security guard had arrived on the platform from which we'd just bolted. We could hear his conversation as he talked into his two-way radio.

"You've gotta get some scientists down here—or some of the techs! This place has been low security ever since it was closed down. I don't know what any of it means . . . it just doesn't look good, I'm telling you! There are all these warning signs flashing!" There was a pause. "One of them says 'potential magnet quench,' whatever that means and the others say 'potential overload danger' . . . Listen, I just work security farther up the line. This isn't even my area! Hurry up and get some brains down here!"

A phone rang and I swung around to Georgia. "You've got a phone! Why didn't you tell me?"

Georgia stood there with the phone in one hand, the other hand opened helplessly as she said, "Cal, it's no use to us. It can only receive incoming calls."

She held the receiver up to her ear for a

moment, but then shook her head. "There's no one there, anyway."

Even before she told me, I knew who had called her. "But it was Damien, wasn't it?"

She nodded. "I think it was meant to be our next instruction. Didn't you get it too?"

I remembered my phone flying out of my hand as I was snatched off the street in Geneva. With the sound of the alarm system blaring in my ears, my suspicions about Georgia started hardening into something more hostile.

"What *is* the next instruction? I'd really like to know because as far as I'm concerned, I haven't been told a thing about this operation except to turn up here."

"That's the weird part," she said, frowning. "There was no instruction. I just heard this weird noise like you get on the line when a fax is starting."

"It might have been interference," I said. "With all the signals and electrical processes going on down here, I wouldn't be surprised."

The computer screens along the wall above the names of the countries started to flash new warnings. "COUNTDOWN TO OVERLOAD COMMENCING NOW" I read on Italy's screen while the others continued to flash their "POTENTIAL OVERLOAD" sign. It looked like Italy was about to be in serious trouble. If SKALD sucked up huge amounts of power, would that knock out the electricity supply in Italy?

I was so scared that Ryan was still in danger. I didn't know whether I was being successful in Damien's mission or not. Maybe I was supposed to get in here and activate SKALD without alerting security. But that would have been impossible and surely Damien would have known that. I had to think! I slid down the wall and slumped to the ground, my brain racing in overdrive, yet at the same time exhausted. I kicked my rucksack out of the way next to Georgia's.

What should my next step be? Should I bang on the door and get arrested?

Then I noticed something. I blinked. Was I seeing things? I stared again. This time there was no doubt. The rucksacks! *They were moving!*

10:38 pm

Startled, I jumped to my feet and then I stared at them, mesmerized. Georgia was staring too, her dark eyes wide in surprise. As we watched, both rucksacks twisted and squirmed as if animals inside were trying to escape. Then, to my astonishment, at exactly the same moment, cuts started appearing in both rucksacks as if someone was cutting a square of the tough fabric from inside the rucksack!

I moved closer, to hear a low, whirring sound coming from inside the rucksacks. Suddenly, I understood what was happening. The self-organizing modbots were cutting their way out! Their shared intelligence had figured out what to do. But what was their goal? Had the signal on Georgia's phone brought them to life?

At almost exactly the same time, a perfectly symmetrical square of fabric fell away from both rucksacks and one by one, the modbots emerged. No longer a jumble of disconnected cubes, the modbots had already connected to each other. Side by side, each set of ten moved along like identical square snakes. I could clearly see the cutting instrument used to saw their way out sticking up on the third cube of each one. Which Melehan number was that, I wondered? Was it M1? Or M4?

"What are they doing?" asked Georgia, moving closer to watch.

The cutting instruments retracted and one of the modbot caterpillars moved forward, heading towards the door. Then it stopped, allowing the second line of modbots to join itself to the first. They now formed a long line of twenty modbots, clunking along, all lights winking, getting closer and closer to the door.

I moved to stop them, but pulled back as I saw the blocks register my proximity and the little harpoons came out of their slits, ready.

At the locked door now, the modbots were climbing on top of each other, stacking up against the door, forming a long column, until they reached the lock just under the handle. I heard the whirring of invisible machinery. I jumped back at a small explosion and a puff of acrid smoke. The door swung open and the sound of the warning sirens became deafening.

"I don't believe it!" Georgia's cry voiced my thoughts exactly. The modbot team had blown the lock!

10:41 pm

From somewhere within the computer system, a computer voice echoed through the cavern, audible above the shrieking alarm.

CRITICAL OVERLOAD! CRITICAL OVERLOAD!

I glanced back at the row of computer screens along the wall. The Italian electricity grid was dark red, flashing—

IMMINENT POWER CRASH ALL SYSTEMS! SHUT DOWN IMMEDIATELY!

I could hear voices yelling in the distance.

"It's got to be shut down! Now! If Italy goes down, France will be next, then Switzerland, then Germany. All of Europe will go dark!"

I didn't have to think too hard to realize what was going on. As SKALD continued to power up, it was draining huge amounts of electricity from the countries around it. One by one, their electricity systems would collapse as all their power was sucked out of them by the enormous energy demands of the seventh experiment! This is what Damien had wanted all along.

This had to be stopped. But how? If the scientists got here and successfully shut down the seventh experiment, Damien would have failed in his plan to cut off Europe's energy supply. And Ryan would die.

Even with these terrible thoughts swirling in my mind, something else was agitating me. Something didn't make sense here. Damien didn't need the modbots to close down Europe's electricity grids. SKALD was doing that job right now.

So what were the modbots for?

Panicked voices reverberated out from the Large Hadron Collider tunnel. It sounded like a group of people heading our way. But I was intent on watching the modbots. They were already moving quickly across the cement platform towards the steel steps that led up to the workstation overhead. They moved in their jerky way up the steel steps, stacking a little to reach each new step, then flattening out again until they'd made their way to the horizontal platform of the workstation—an oversized, cuboid caterpillar. There they started marching across the steel of the floor in the direction of the computers. I followed them, keeping a safe distance away.

COUNTDOWN TO FATAL OVERLOAD:
SHUTDOWN IN 3:04 MINUTES
FINAL CRITICAL OVERLOAD WARNING

The modbots, closer now to the long lab bench that held the computers, were organizing something new. Something now protruded from the lead modbot. I couldn't make it out from where I stood so I raced up the steel steps two at a time. As I got closer I saw what it was, and several puzzling thoughts came together and made sense. It was a USB and the modbots were heading for the nearest computer.

I heard Boges's voice in my head. *Just imagine it, dude! A hundred and seventy computing centers in thirty-six different countries! The biggest supercomputer system in the world!*

The modbot marked M1 must be the cube loaded with the Mordred virus—and it was about to upload the virus into a computer connected with over a hundred and fifty computer centers, connecting tens of thousands of other computers in thirty-six different countries! Hundreds of thousands of computers all over the world and all infected with a virus worse than Stuxnet!

I had to stop it!

But then I remembered—if I foiled Damien's plan, and saved millions of people, Ryan would die. I was paralyzed by the enormity of my decision. How could I not do it? But how could I kill my own brother?

The modbot snake was climbing, the USB on a fine steel arm aiming for the nearest computer port. I had no choice, I had to do this. I'd have to figure out a way of saving Ryan afterwards. SI-6 would help. They'd find a way of making Damien believe that the Mordred file virus had been successfully loaded into the world's biggest computer system.

I hesitated. If I stopped the modbots, would Damien know immediately? There might not be time to save Ryan—I would save the world and lose my brother!

I couldn't do it. And yet, the terrifying scenario of worldwide power failure resulting in thousands, maybe tens of thousands, of people dying in riots or perishing for lack of heat or ventilators or . . . I saw Ryan's face in my mind; I knew what he would say.

Do it. Save the world, bro.

My mind was made up. I could only hope there was still time to save him.

Forgive me, Ryan.

10:43 pm

I raced towards the modbot snake which had now reached the top of the lab bench. Another few moments and it would push the USB home into the computer's port.

The screaming siren moved up into a louder, more urgent tone. I could hear what sounded like a small battalion of soldiers thudding towards us!

I picked up a swivel chair and smashed it down onto the modbots. They broke in half, but within moments, they had reassembled. A burst of flame ignited from one of the narrow slits in the second modbot cube, missing my face by inches as I tripped against the lab bench and fell backward.

I sprang back up as the modbots continued their relentless progress towards the computer port. This time, I used the chair sideways, to swipe them off the bench top. But they regrouped even faster this time, completely undamaged. *What were they made of?*

I raised the chair again, but before I inflicted as much damage as I could, I was tackled from behind. I hit the deck hard and the swivel chair crashed on top of me.

"What do you think you're doing?" I screamed at Georgia.

"Protecting the modbots!" Georgia screamed. "Don't you understand? If we can shut down the electrical grid, we can save the world from pollution!"

She'd pinned me down squarely and I could barely move or breathe.

"Georgia!" I begged. "The modbots are going to load a virus. The SKALD experiment alone is enough to destroy the electrical grids and this is far worse! This is about destroying all the computers in the world. Just think what that means. There are millions of lives at stake!" I struggled to get out of her grip, but she had me.

"You're lying!" she cried. "Damien wants to help the world! He only wants to threaten it just to make people wake up and see the damage they're causing. As soon as the governments promise to give him what he wants, he's going to use the Arthur key to reverse Mordred's damage!"

My worst suspicions were confirmed—Georgia had swallowed Damien's lies completely. There could be no reasoning with her.

"GET OFF ME!" I yelled in her face as I looked up and saw the small steel arm line itself up to deliver the Mordred virus into the computer port beside it. As I struggled, I noticed Georgia had what looked like a silver pen in her hand. She nodded. "That's right, you know what this is, Cal. Don't make me use it, because I will."

It was the stinger spray!

It was the impetus I needed to channel all my strength into one final push, and levering off the bench leg, I managed to roll over and pin Georgia to the ground, knocking the silver tube from her hand.

Leaping up, I tried to dash the steel arm away. But it was too late! I got badly stung, but barely felt it as I watched in horror as the steel arm rammed forward into the USB port. The Mordred key virus, the worst virus in the history of civilization, had just been loaded into the world's computers!

Uselessly, I yelled out, *"No! NO!"*

10:44 pm

Suddenly everything stopped. The sirens fell silent. The flashing warnings dissolved back into black screens. The digital countdown clocks froze.

The Mordred virus must have started spreading already, closing down everything. This could be the end of the world, a little voice in my head said. Ryan, Mum, Gabbi . . . *I'm so sorry.*

I stopped worrying about Georgia. There was no need to try to stop her now. The damage had been done. A huge smile split her pointed face and her eyes shone as she got to her feet, brushing herself down. "You don't even understand how important this is. No more pollution. The earth can be healed. Imagine how wonderful that will be!"

"Are you completely *insane?*" I yelled, grabbing her hard by the shoulders and looking into her fanatical eyes. I wanted to slap her across the face and bring her to her senses!

Beneath us, the squad of security guards had arrived and spread out along the platform.

I had failed completely. And now I was about to be arrested. What would become of Ryan? A voice calling my name cut through my despairing thoughts.

"Cal! Cal!"

Huh?

Standing on the cement platform below me was the last man in the world I ever expected to see here. "*Dr. Freeman?*" I asked, bewildered. "What are you doing here? How did you . . ?"

Dazed and confused, I slumped back against the lab bench. "What's going on? I don't understand," I finally whispered.

Dr. Freeman walked up the steel steps towards me. "Cal . . . it's all right. Everything is going to be OK. I've remembered who I am—I'm Dr. Jeffrey Thoroughgood. I know what's going on here. I helped design the Mordred key virus. I also worked on SKALD. Boges contacted me to see if I could help and told me you were heading for Geneva. That told me everything I needed to know. I alerted the authorities and here we are."

"But it's too late . . ." I began to say looking across to where the modbots had become dormant again, after delivering their deadly payload into the computer.

"Watch this," Jeffrey said confidently. He pulled out a remote device and the modbots woke up. As I watched, open-mouthed in astonishment, Jeffrey tapped at the remote buttons and the modbots started to reorganize themselves until the second-to-last cube in the long line was now at the front. The new lead modbot produced a steel arm loaded with a USB just like the previous leader had. Sensing an empty port, this steel arm pushed this second USB into the computer port.

"I've just loaded the Arthur key. It will undo

any damage when the system is switched back on again in a few moments."

Georgia was weeping quietly, curled up on the floor. "You've spoiled everything," she cried, like a child.

"Spoiled everything? You completely betrayed me," I said. "Pretending to be my friend, pretending to be here to help me. You were sent by Damien to make sure that I did the job."

I turned back to Dr. Thoroughgood. "Damien has my brother, Ryan," I whispered. "I'm just so frightened he'll be hurt now that Damien's plan has been stopped."

"Don't worry, Cal. We're going to track down that monster of a brother of mine. And we're going to find Ryan." His face set with determination. "Ever flown in a Learjet?" he asked.

Swiss Countryside

11:15 pm

Dr. Thoroughgood had explained to the authorities what had happened while I'd waited impatiently. I had forced myself to keep calm even though every tick of the clock reminded me that Ryan was still in danger. But I was also mentally and physically exhausted, almost unable to move. Georgia had just kept sobbing and then looking at me angrily.

I couldn't imagine how Dr. Thoroughgood managed it, but not much later, we were permitted to leave the SKALD precinct. I didn't trust Georgia at all and didn't take my eyes off her, watching her intently. Dr. Thoroughgood had a car waiting and within minutes the three of us were being driven through the night.

I borrowed Dr. Thoroughgood's phone to call Boges and tried to give him a short version of what had happened.

"I've got about a million questions I want to ask you, but right now, dude, I'll keep it brief. Repro's checked out Science Valley. We thought maybe Oriana was keeping Ryan there, but we were wrong. We haven't got a clue as to where he is. I'm sorry," Boges said.

I called Winter.

"Thank goodness you called! I've been going out of my mind with worry. What's happened? Where are you? Have you found Ryan?"

"Call Boges for an update. I'll be back as soon as the jet can get us there. Dr. Freeman turned out to be Dr. Jeffrey Thoroughgood, Damien's brother." I heard her gasp of astonishment all the way down the line. After a pause I said, "Winter, who's Grendel?"

"Grendel? Isn't he a character from some ancient poem?" Winter said.

"Damien sent me picture of Ryan and a message that said that Ryan will meet Grendel."

"I'm on it, OK? Get some rest on your way back. There's nothing you can do while you're in the air and you'll need your strength to help us save Ryan," she added.

"I will. Well, I'll try. And please try to find out what you can. Whatever Grendel is, you can bet it isn't good." As I hung up, I couldn't get the countdown above Ryan's head out of my mind. *What had happened when it reached zero?* Somehow I needed to bargain for Ryan's life. If I still could.

I looked out the window and saw that we were pulling up at a private airfield. The driver drove straight to a large hangar where a gleaming Learjet 60 stood, with its distinctive delta tail fins. Georgia whimpered beside me.

"My arm is hurting," she complained.

I was struggling to feel sorry for her. She'd turned into my enemy at the last moment, but it was obvious she'd been completely brainwashed by Damien. I wondered about the contents of the Biosurge implant. Maybe the performance-enhancing herbs weren't so healthy after all. I'd heard that weight lifters and athletes sometimes went crazy from using dangerous supplements.

Swiss Airspace

<u>**11:51 pm**</u>

Dr. Thoroughgood's driver turned out to also be his pilot so it wasn't long before we were on board. I sank back into one of the luxurious leather recliner seats and buckled up, and Georgia, still complaining of her sore arm, sat across the aisle. Past the walnut paneling, I could see into the cockpit and watched as the pilot went through the preflight routine with Dr. Jeffrey acting as First Officer. One day, I hoped to have my own Learjet.

The two Pratt and Whitney turbofans spun into action and we were airborne very quickly and climbing fast. Normally, I'd be rapt at the thought of having a ride in a Learjet, and I'd be up in the cockpit, talking to the pilot. But the fate of my brother was all I could think of at the moment—that and the confusing events of the last twenty-four hours.

Once we were at cruising altitude, Dr. Jeffrey left the cockpit for a while and came to sit with me.

"You know that Damien kidnapped my brother, Ryan," I said. "That's the only reason I was there. I didn't mean to activate SKALD. Damien threatened to kill Ryan if I didn't carry out his orders." I paused for a moment and thought. "I'm really pleased that you've regained your memory. But right now, all I can think of is Ryan." I sighed deeply. Sleep was trying to force its way in, but my mind still raced.

"Cal, I do understand. I meant what I said about helping you find him. I'm so sorry your family has been caught up in this. I always knew that my brother resented my success with my inventions. Instead of working alongside me, he became greedy, and filled with envy and hatred. It seems that he planned to get rid of me, but he couldn't quite bring himself to kill me so instead he locked me up on that island. I guess he hoped I'd just die there and then he could simply take over everything. He's pretty much done that already. I've had a look at the deeds of some of my properties, and they're no longer in my name, but his. Everything I own appears to belong to my brother. He must have forged documents to do all this."

"But how come you forgot everything?" I asked.

"Damien added mind-altering drugs to my food and water. I'm lucky that I didn't go completely insane with such a dangerous mixture of chemicals. My mind was completely scrambled for a long time and it took me weeks to be free of the effects of the drugs."

I looked across at Georgia, my doubts about the Biosurge implant turning into real suspicion. Damien hadn't hesitated to use drugs to destroy his brother's mind.

"Damien was always jealous," Dr. Thoroughgood was saying. "I should have known he would go over the edge. All my work, properties . . . my inventions. Even my robotic animals."

"I've met some of those," I said, "the spythons on Shadow Island, and the vicious cat that was guarding his office."

Jeffrey nodded. "I designed and made a dog too, which went missing some time ago. I worked with the military and other government experts to create Mordred, the most complex and destructive virus ever created. But it was only ever intended as a deterrent or a last-resort measure. We designed the Arthur key, so as to always have the antidote which could be swiftly applied once the point had been made. Damien discovered what I was doing and no doubt decided he would use the Mordred key in the worst possible way—to blackmail the governments of countries by threatening to unleash Mordred on all their utilities and companies unless they paid him astronomical amounts of money. He doesn't want to earn wealth, he wants to take it—like a common thief."

"Like Mordred overthrew the rightful King Arthur," I said, remembering what Winter had researched. "I found a list," I said, "in the laboratory, with all these numbers and the name Melehan. Boges said they were ID names and numbers for different electronic devices."

"He was right. Each of those was the name and number of each individual modbot. Depending on how they were programmed, some were repair bots, some were attack bots, others were cutting bots. But there was only one cube programmed with the Mordred key. It had no other capacity than delivering the virus. I gave that one the value of zero. Nothing. Because there's nothing retrievable left on the hard drive once Mordred gets going . . ."

I recalled the listing: Mordred_0.

A shocking moan from Georgia interrupted us. It was clear she was in serious pain.

"What is it?" I asked, bending over her as she rocked backward and forward, noticing how her upper arm was inflamed and swollen. I wondered if I'd hurt her tackling her earlier. But somehow, I didn't think so.

"I feel hot. My arm hurts," she groaned.

"I don't like the look of that," said Jeffrey as he gently took hold of Georgia's arm. He examined the infected area.

"It's the implant," she said. "It's really hurting." She was becoming more feverish and restless, unable to get comfortable in the luxurious seat.

"It must be the Biosurge," I said.

"What's Biosurge?" he asked.

"Boges was having it analyzed," I said, "but we hadn't had any results back yet. I think Damien was using some kind of drug just like he used on you, Jeffrey. Something to make Georgia crazy enough to swallow everything he said." I told him about Travis and the Johannesburg Zenith operative who had to go to the hospital as well. "Georgia is the third person to suddenly fall ill." I remembered how Oriana de la Force had injected me with a small bug under the skin and how it had become infected before my dear old great-uncle Bart had dug it out for me.

DAY 0

0 days left . . .

European Airspace

12:36 am

Georgia's condition was deteriorating fast. She was becoming incoherent, struggling and muttering. From out of one of the walnut-paneled compartments, Dr. Thoroughgood pulled out a professional first-aid kit.

He looked at me, face very serious. "Cal, you're going to have to assist me. I'm going to take out that implant right now. This seems like a very dangerous infection. Here, wash your hands."

We cleaned our hands with hospital antiseptic and Dr. Thoroughgood cleaned the angry red skin on Georgia's upper arm.

By now, Georgia was unconscious. I watched as Dr. Thoroughgood sprayed the inflamed area with a local anesthetic and passed me some thick cotton swabbing from the first-aid kit. He made a straight, deep cut along the side of the scar on her upper arm. Bright-red blood sprang from the cut and I quickly mopped it up with the swabbing. Dr. Thoroughgood gently probed the wound with tweezers and carefully lifted out a small bloody object. He poured some methylated spirits into a container and dropped the bloody implant into it.

I watched while Dr. Thoroughgood expertly stitched up the precise wound. "We'll get her straight to a hospital once we land back home."

"Surgery and robotic design," I said. "You sure are good with both. I've met your robot dog and cat—and they were both pretty impressive." I remembered something else. "In the laboratory, there were glass jars with strange little creatures in them. I thought they were Irukandji jellyfish, but they were the wrong shape."

"Another one of my little eccentricities," said Dr. Jeffrey. "They are tiny cyborgs—a hybrid of cybernetic and organic cells. They're a mix of silicone combined with the pulsing heart cells of a rat. Damien was always fascinated by them."

"He extracted the toxin from jellyfish," I said, telling him about the stinging spray he'd given the Zenith team members. As I spoke, I yawned and stood up to stretch. My jetlag washed over me in a tidal rush and I sat down again abruptly.

"Rest now, Cal. There's no more to be done

till we get there. And you'll need to be fresh for whatever comes next. I'll wake you when we arrive home, don't worry." Jeffrey smiled kindly.

"OK, maybe I'll just close my eyes for a few minutes," I agreed. I hated to rest while Ryan was still in danger, but it made sense to save my energy for what was to come.

Albion Harbor Private Airfield
Home

7:31 am

At last, after a night landing in Manila to refuel, we landed back home the next morning. Georgia was sleeping heavily as if her body, exhausted from fighting the infection, was now catching up with much-needed rest. At the airport, an ambulance was waiting to take her away for tests and observation.

I was pleased to see Boges and Winter, together with Sophie and BB, waiting for us at the terminal, but I couldn't really rejoice, not with Ryan still missing. I was shaking with the intensity of wanting to move, to find Ryan.

Dr. Thoroughgood and BB began a hurried conversation while Winter threw her arms around me and squeezed me hard. Boges patted me so thoroughly that he almost winded me.

"We contacted SI-6 right after you called us," said Winter. "The police are hoping to get some leads on where Damien might be holding Ryan."

"Dad said he will put every resource into it," Sophie added.

"You'll need to," said Jeffrey who had caught up with us. "Did Damien say anything, anything at all to you, Cal, in that last conversation you had with him that might give us a clue?"

I racked my brains, trying to recall the threats made by the sneering man on the beach back on Shadow Island as he'd held a gun to Ryan. "I can't think now," I said, mentally drained by everything that had happened overseas.

"Get back to your family now, Cal," BB advised as he readied to leave with Sophie. "Leave this to us. We've got everyone on the job to help us find Ryan and Damien."

In spite of BB's encouraging words, uneasy memories were surfacing and troubling me. Memories of the robotic dog who'd first given me the coded message that had started the whole huge operation.

"Have you discovered who the mole is, BB?" I asked as we reached the exit.

BB sighed. "It's a big organization, Cal. I'm afraid we don't know who it is yet."

"Where did you get the robot dog from?" I

asked. "The one that delivered the message to me?"

"It belongs to Paddy," said BB. "Using the robot dog was his idea. Why do you ask?"

Jeffrey said the robot dog had "gone missing" some time ago . . .

Disconnected bits of information started to join up in my mind. "Somebody knew when D'Merrick was arriving on Shadow Island," I said. "Somebody betrayed her. Only a handful of people knew about that."

"Even I didn't know about it until well after the event," said BB, frowning.

I knew I was on the right track now. "The person I spoke to said he would pass information on to you immediately. But they didn't, did they?"

BB stopped mid-stride and frowned. "I had no idea you'd been in contact with anyone else from SI-6 while you were on the island."

I suddenly got the whole thing. Someone in SI-6 was a friend of Damien's, in fact, so closely involved that he'd managed to get hold of one of the robotic animals stolen from Jeffrey—the robotic dog. He'd lied to me when he said he would pass the information on to BB.

"Tell me, Cal. Who did you speak to?" BB said quickly.

"Paddy."

BB pulled out his phone and made a call. "Issue a warrant against Patrick McManus. He is to be immediately isolated. Seize his computer and all his files."

I didn't wait to hear any more as BB got into his car. As I turned to Boges, I heard a phone chime. "Whose is that?" I asked.

Boges pulled a phone out of his pocket and looked at it as he said, "It's Ryan's."

I read the message as Boges's face whitened. Then I grabbed Jeffrey's arm. "Jeffrey! We *must* find Ryan. Now! Look at this!" I said.

▯ My brother puts $15 million into this Cayman Islands account in one hour or your brother dies. Very horribly . . . you can count on that.

Details of a bank account followed the message. This was for real.

Our shocked eyes met. "Cal, we need to get BB back," Jeffrey said. "We have to tell SI-6 and the police about this!" He pulled out his phone and I grabbed it from his hand.

"No way! We can't risk Ryan's life. Don't you see that a police operation would be too slow. By the time they organize and get there, Ryan will be dead, and if he isn't, the minute Damien hears police sirens or sees any police, he'll die then! You once said you'd do anything for me. You mustn't call the police." I looked at my watch. 7:52 a.m. *I had sixty minutes to save my brother's life.*

It didn't take long for Jeffrey to make up his mind. "I owe you my freedom—my life. I'll authorize the money transfer now."

"Thank you! But we still have to find Ryan; we can't trust Damien to release him. So think— *think!* Where would Damien be holding him?" I begged.

I felt Winter's steadying arm around my shoulders and was aware of Boges's close presence.

"I've already given the addresses of my properties to the police. They sent local officers out to check them. They found nothing at any of them," Jeffrey said.

"But they don't understand the urgency of the situation," I said.

"There's really nowhere I can think of . . ." He paused, his face gaunt with worry and frustration. Then I noticed his expression change. "Wait, there *is* one place I didn't even think to mention because it's a ruin."

"What place?" I asked feverishly.

"It was our grandparents' place. It was badly damaged in a fire years ago. It got its name because of its high position which made it one of the first signs of civilization that sailors saw when they were coming home. It was called *Land Sighting.*"

Like the tumbling colored fragments in a kaleidoscope suddenly stopping and locking into a complex pattern, words, images and understanding came together in my head. When his brain was scrambled, Jeffrey had talked about a dream, of something called land sighting and I'd thought he was just wandering in his mind. I recalled what Damien said on the beach, his contempt for everybody, how he boasted that he would hear all about the success of his egotistical plan later, "*at land sighting where no one can possibly find . . .*"

I had thought he simply meant somewhere off the mainland. But he was going to be waiting at Land Sighting where he believed nobody could possibly find him. *Him, my brother, Ryan—and Grendel.*

"That's it! I know where Ryan is! Dr. Jeffrey, you said you'd help me. We've got to take the Learjet to Land Sighting *now!*"

7:54 am

We raced back to the airfield to find the pilot checking the Learjet. A few words from Jeffrey and we were strapping in for takeoff. Fifteen minutes later, we were at 43,000 feet and on our way north.

On the way, Dr. Jeffrey took Ryan's phone and texted back.

▊ I will do as you say. Electronic transfer of this size will take some time. I can't do it by then. You must extend the deadline.

Almost immediately came the reply.

▊ Extension denied.

Jeffrey started making frantic calls to arrange the transfer.

"Cal," said Winter, from where she sat opposite me, "I hate telling you this, but I did as you asked and researched Grendel." She took a deep breath before continuing, "Grendel is a very nasty piece of work. He's a monster—half human, half demon. He features in an old English poem from the seventh century. He rips warriors apart."

I shuddered, remembering Damien's terrible threat. "What has some character in an ancient poem got to do with threatening my brother?" I asked, not wanting to think about it.

"You could say the same about Arthur and Mordred," she said. "Jeffrey seems to have a bit of a soft spot for early literature."

Time was running out for Ryan and my imagination was running away with me as I pictured Grendel. I couldn't stand it any longer. I hurried up to where Jeffrey was sitting just as he hung up his phone.

"Tell me about Grendel," I said.

"Normally, I'd say there's nothing to be worried about. Grendel was an experimental robot I used for research reasons, but he also used to bring me tea and play chess. Grendel is programmed according to Asimov's laws of robotics—never to harm a human. But in Damien's hands . . ." His voice trailed off. "Cal, it pains me to admit this, but my brother is clearly a ruthless and remorseless man."

Damien had subverted every good program that his brother had created, turning helpful robotics into attack systems. I hated to think how he might have programmed Grendel.

As the Learjet speared through the stratosphere, I brought Boges's laptop to Jeffrey who pulled up images of gargoyles and showed one to me. "This is the gargoyle that I copied when I made Grendel," he said. "I made an almost-perfect robotic version of him. When he stands tall, he's over six feet high."

I swallowed hard. Grendel was a hunched, brooding creature, half demon, half human, with a dog's face and horns, with malevolent and stony eyes. His overlong sinewy arms ended in almost human hands except for the ferocious talons growing at the ends of his fingers. I looked at Jeffrey as if to ask—*why?*

He didn't have an answer for that, but I could hardly blame him for the situation we now found ourselves in. Damien and Oriana were the only people responsible for this nightmare.

Land Sighting
Mount Astley

8:45 am

We'd landed at a local airfield a few miles from Land Sighting. Jeffrey had organized for a car to be waiting for us and we had sped away as soon as we'd touched down. After a few minutes' drive, we found the half-burned sign hanging off heavy-duty metal mesh gates. We had arrived at Land Sighting.

We left the vehicle and the driver near the gate. We crept along the short dirt road to the burned-out ruins. The place was still standing, but only just—visible against the skyline on the high ridge, but as we approached, keeping our flashlights low, it was clear that there were floorboards missing from the wide front verandah. A broken padlock and chain hung uselessly from the front door, which was ajar. Silently, I pushed it open. It creaked in a spooky way and I stepped inside, shining my flashlight around.

"The place looks completely empty," I whispered back to Jeffrey. Winter and Boges stepped inside too and the four of us looked around the room. Burned walls with water stains and derelict floors still stank of the smell of fire.

Curiously though, in one corner was a square of carpet with two luxurious sofas in front of a massive plasma screen, a bar cabinet to one side of it and a pile of action-movie DVDs on the other. Was this where Oriana and Damien relaxed after a hard day's evil? I wondered.

Ahead of us was a staircase leading down into total blackness. I played my flashlight beam over the steps, but that only revealed as far as the first turn.

"Careful, dude," Boges warned. "We don't know what's down there."

"There's a good chance that Ryan is down there. I'm going," I said, moving towards the first step.

"Careful, Cal. This could be a trap." Winter placed a restraining hand on my arm.

"Trap or not," I said, looking at my watch, "Ryan has only four minutes until Damien releases Grendel."

"If you're going, I'm coming too," said Winter.

"And me," said Boges, without enthusiasm.

"What if he's got that gun?" I whispered.

"I've brought the Catnap," said Boges. "I just have to get close enough to him to use it. He'll drop like a brick."

8:48 am

The four of us crept down the stairs until we came to what looked like a cellar door. I opened it very slowly and looked around. To my complete amazement, it opened onto a well-equipped, very long and well-lit laboratory, much better fitted out than the smaller lab on Shadow Island. With every cell of my being on red alert, I stepped in with the others following closely behind. The opposite wall seemed to be made of black glass and right at the end of the long lab bench was a very large beaker with tiny cyborgs pulsing around in the fluid.

Winter was right beside me and I whispered, "There are cyborgs in that beaker. Could be useful?"

Jeffrey added, "I wouldn't be surprised if Damien has made them deadly too."

Winter glanced at them and nodded, when without any warning, we were plunged into darkness.

"Hey!" Winter cried.

As my vision improved, it took me a few seconds to figure out what I was looking at. At the end of the laboratory, what I'd thought was a black glass wall was actually some kind of two-way black glass because a light had come on in the far right corner, allowing me to see Ryan, handcuffed and miserable, sitting on a low stool. He seemed to have no idea about our presence and I was about to call out to him and run to him when I felt a hand on my arm.

"Just wait," said Jeffrey. "I'll go first. Damien must be close by and I might be able to reason with him."

"No," I said. "He's well beyond being reasoned with. And he already knows we're here."

Almost before I'd finished speaking, another light came on, illuminating what lay behind the left-hand side of the black glass dividing wall.

I stared in horror.

Grendel!

8:51 am

Towering over six feet tall, he was far worse than the gargoyle that Jeffrey had shown me on the jet. This Grendel looked like some kind of human reptile, with his ugly snouted face and horns, long skinny arms ending in deadly looking claws, and thick, heavy, clawed hindquarters.

A sound from behind us made me swing around. A light flashed on to reveal Damien, his face full of malice, his eyes glaring with fury, his pistol trained on us. And right behind him, the unmistakable figure of Oriana de la Force, red hair gleaming in the light, her eyes narrowed with malevolent intent.

"How wonderful!" she exulted. "Now we've got the whole tribe of little interferers, our band of save-the-world fools! This will be the last time I ever have to see your ugly faces!"

"You'll never get away with it!" I said.

"It's quite a bonanza," sneered Damien, "and what a story it'll make in the press. Mad scientist's robot goes mad—kills creator and four intruders. That's if they ever find you down here."

"As for me, I'll be trying out my new bikini on a beach in the Bahamas," Oriana added. She hesitated only a moment. "Those millions are in our bank account by now, aren't they, Damien?"

I saw Boges edging uneasily closer, trying to get into position with his Catnap tube.

"This is better than I expected," Damien snarled, ignoring Oriana's question. "Finally I can get rid of you too, dear big brother." Then he turned his rage on Boges and Winter. "And you'll be very sorry that you ever knew the Ormond twins."

He backed us towards the far end of the laboratory. Ryan had jumped to his feet when the lights behind Damien came on.

"Ryan!" I called out.

My brother ran to the glass wall that separated us and bashed it with his handcuffed hands. "Cal! Cal! Get me out of here!"

I could see from the unfocused way he was looking through the glass that he couldn't see me, only hear me. I was desperately looking for a way through the glass wall when Damien poked me painfully with his pistol.

"Get back!" he commanded. "Get back now!"

"Damien, please—" Jeffrey started to say, but Damien turned on his brother, hitting him hard over the head with the butt of the pistol. Jeffrey staggered back and slid down against the nearby lab bench, unconscious. Winter ran to him, but Damien snapped a command, "Get back or you'll get the same treatment."

Reluctantly, Winter drew back, but I saw her eyeballing the beaker on the bench above Jeffrey.

With a nasty grin on his face, Damien pushed us closer and closer to the glass wall. That's when I realized that Ryan still hadn't seen Grendel, who was hidden behind the opaque separating wall.

"You thought you'd ruin everything for me," said Damien. "But I've got nothing to lose now. I did a little fiddling with my brother's programming. Grendel will attack the first human in his path as soon as he comes online. And then another and then another. He's like the Terminator. He sees a human—he goes after them! He just keeps coming at you and he's almost impossible to destroy."

Oriana clapped her hands with glee, scarlet fingernails flashing. "I've always loved action movies! This will be a thousand times more fun!"

I stared again at the horrifying sight of the robotic monster, the dead cold eyes, the terrible ripping talons, the wolf-like fangs and the devilish horns. It was like some medieval nightmare come to life!

"Grendel will first kill Ryan and then he will come for all of you!" Damien laughed.

With that, the glass wall separating us from both Ryan and Grendel slid back. Ryan, for the first time could see us. He came running towards us, but then he saw Damien approaching with the pistol.

"Stay where you are," Damien snarled. He looked at his watch and sneered. "Oops. *Time's up.*"

8:52 am

The opaque dividing wall between Grendel and Ryan also slid back and for the first time Ryan saw Jeffrey's monster.

"What is that?" Ryan yelled, his face showing

the same terror and horror that I knew was etched on mine.

At the same time, Damien grabbed Ryan, pushing him forward right into the path of the monster. I flew at him, but he hit me hard with the pistol handle and I fell to the floor, dazed and shocked. The next few seconds were total confusion as I tried to regain my balance. There was a low whirring sound as the monstrous robot booted up. Its eyes glowed red. Its mouth opened, revealing rows of sharp metal teeth. Blinding beams shone from its eyes. It reared up, raising its vicious talons, aiming straight for Ryan!

Ryan was trapped—Damien was behind him and the robotic monstrosity was advancing menacingly. It brought one of its steel claws down in a slashing motion, and then the other, its horned wolf's head focused on my brother's chest, just inches away.

"Give me the Catnap!" I yelled to Boges, snatching it from his hand. Grendel raised both slashing talons high again, ready to bring them down to tear my brother to pieces. With a stabbing action I lunged forward and jabbed Ryan with the Catnap.

"Cal! What are you doing?" Boges screamed.

Ryan dropped like a piece of lead and the slashing talons of Grendel propelled forward over the collapsed body of my brother, ripping through the head, chest and belly of Damien Thoroughgood. He screamed and floundered, bleeding everywhere at once, the pistol flying from his hand and sliding across the floor.

Boges, moving faster than I'd ever seen, leapt forward and kicked the pistol away. As Oriana lunged forward to grab it, Winter sloshed the beaker full of cyborgs all over her!

Oriana's shrieks stopped almost as soon as they started. Jeffrey was right to guess that Damien had made them deadly too. The shock of dozens of fatal doses of Irukandji venom hit her, killing her outright. Her body convulsed— once, twice, and then stopped, her face frozen in a snarl of pain. And with that, Oriana de la Force was no more.

But Grendel kept coming after us, relentlessly, its huge hindquarters thundering with each step, building up speed.

We didn't wait. I grabbed my brother and together with Boges and Winter, hauled him and Jeffrey to their feet and dragged them out of the lab, slamming the door behind us. We could hear Grendel coming after us, hammering at the laboratory door, breaking through.

"Hurry up!" I yelled, looking back. "Grendel's gotten through the door! You've got to go faster!"

But it was impossible. We were hampered by Jeffrey's and Ryan's dead weight.

"Keep going!" I shouted at Winter and Boges as they hauled Jeffrey and Ryan up the last steps and into the ruined living room. "Get to the car. I'll delay Grendel somehow!"

"But how, Cal? He's impossible to stop!" Winter's face was distraught as she paused in her efforts to help Boges lift Ryan and Jeffrey towards the doorway.

Boges said nothing, but his face told me everything—*the situation is hopeless, dude.*

"Just get out! Get to the car!" I shouted.

Grendel was almost at the top of the stairs. Already, he'd fixed his demon red eyes on me as the others finally got away through the door and outside into the night.

Now I had to face Grendel alone. He was coming at me, great talons poised to rip me apart. How could I stop him? I fumbled around for something to hit him with.

Uselessly, I picked up the television remote, thinking maybe if I threw it at his face it might give me a few seconds in which to think of something smarter. The massive screen lit up behind me as the television came on and in its flashing light, Grendel gleamed diabolically. He was almost upon me when suddenly I stumbled and fell backward against the plasma screen, rolling sideways to escape Grendel's talons. But it was too late! His claws rose higher to rip me open.

Down they came. But the fiendish talons crashed through the screen. I was showered with broken glass as I scrambled out of the way. Any second now and I'd be ripped to pieces! But it didn't happen. Grendel was going after the moving figures on the huge screen!

When Grendel's second talon smashed down through the insides of the ruined television screen, a loud explosion erupted. I backed away in fear, but was unable to tear my eyes away as the robot started to short circuit. Then Grendel and the plasma screen, inextricably entwined, both exploded in a blinding shower of sparks.

The human figures on the large television screen had fooled Grendel's biometric scanning eyes!

He'd gone for them instead of me! I shouted out loud with relief. Ryan was safe, everyone was safe and Grendel was a mess of smashed electronics and leathery skin, twitching and sparking on the floor. I jumped around like a crazy thing, yelling and punching the smoky air. I doubled over and laughed and laughed until tears rolled down my face.

Outside, I could hear sirens.

Epilogue

We had driven together to SI-6 to meet BB and the others for our final debrief.

On the way, Ryan had filled us in about what had happened after Oriana grabbed him at Science Valley.

"She jumped me with that robot cat and before I knew what had happened, I was drugged and woke up down in the lab in handcuffs."

"I almost didn't save you in time," I said, not able to look Ryan in the eye.

"But you *did*," he said. "And you made the right decision in Geneva, don't worry." He hugged me tight.

As we walked down the corridor at SI-6, Winter handed me an envelope.

"This came for you. I picked it up at your mum's place."

The letter was from Indonesia. Frowning, I ripped it open. I didn't recognize the handwriting.

I feel bad about the way everything turned out. Damien saved my life once and I felt I owed him a lot. But then it got too much for me. It just wasn't right—I wasn't sure what he was planning, he kept things from me, but I knew it wasn't good. When I realized the Psycho Kid's twin was on the island, I sent you the countdown pic hoping you'd come to Shadow Island and put a stop to what Damien was doing somehow. It was me who took the photograph of you and Ryan together just in case I needed something over you. I made up the riddle about where to look in the cemetery for the key. Now I'm just going to blend in with the locals and do some fishing. If you're ever in Surabaya, maybe look me up.

Hamish

"It was Hamish all along!" I said. "I never suspected it was him."

"Dr. Jeffrey Thoroughgood has recovered from the nasty gash on his head," said BB as we strode into the interview room—from which Paddy was distinctly absent, although I was pleased to see D'Merrick and Axel at the table. "He's considering what he'll do next."

I glanced at my friends. "That's good to hear. Maybe he should leave creating robotic animals alone for a while."

BB continued, "You'll be happy to hear that both Travis and Georgia are almost fully recovered from the aftereffects of Biosurge and Shadow Island is off limits to everyone for some time—that volcano is still very active. Our drones show that the whole resort has been covered in ash." His expression became more serious. "And Damien Thoroughgood and Oriana de la Force are dead."

I nodded, silent.

He turned to Boges and said, "Thank you for getting the results of the chemical analysis on Biosurge forwarded on to me. Whether or not it enhanced athletic performance, I have no idea," he continued drily, "but it certainly contained a concoction that would scramble anybody's brains eventually, and also have dire physical consequences."

"So it's true," I said. "Georgia didn't understand the consequences of what she was doing."

"According to the analysis, it was a cocktail of things that should never have been put together, let alone implanted in people. Police authorities all over the world have been alerted to it and all the Zenith team operatives have had the implants removed. A number of them were already very ill."

He paused, looking serious. "Agent Flint tells me that with Boges's help, she was able to get into the sealed orders website and that gave us the targets. We contacted Interpol and that's how we were able to pick up each Zenith team operative as they moved in to carry out their mission. Boges will be getting a special commendation from us, as you all will, of course."

"It was a team effort," I said.

BB smiled broadly. "Cal, we couldn't have done this without you and your willingness to go to any lengths to discover the truth."

BB, Axel and D'Merrick walked the four of us to the entrance foyer of SI-6. I wondered how long it would take them to recover from the terrible shock of Paddy's betrayal.

"You'll be pleased to hear," said D'Merrick, "that Jeffrey's robot dog and cat are going to the Robotics Engineering Museum." She swung her braid back, turning to Axel. "We're really going to miss you guys. Aren't we, Axel?"

"And so will I," said a beautiful young woman, emerging from her office as we walked past. "'Specially you, Boges."

Boges turned bright-red as he introduced us, and Winter gave him a meaningful nudge. "This is Maxine—Maxine Flint." Maxine joined us as we walked towards the main foyer. Through the glass doors, I could see Sophie talking to the security guy outside, and the grin on my brother's face got wider. Ryan must have called her to meet us.

Axel smiled as we paused a moment in front of the doors. "Maybe you'll work for us again, Cal?"

The four of us linked arms—Ryan, Winter, me and Boges—as the double doors swung open and we walked through. Sophie ran up to join us, linking arms with Ryan. It was so good that all of us were together again, safe and on our way home. Back to a normal life and hanging out together.

On the top step, I turned back. "You've got to be kidding!" I grinned.